Before I met Longinus, I knew only three things:

First, I was a slave at a Roman Laundry with no hope of escape.

Second, my small stature and unfortunate anatomy meant I must passively submit to the wanton desires of the Roman citizens and slaves.

Third, I would never know love.

Longinus proved I was wrong in all respects.

Formosus Petrus, through family misfortune, has become a young slave in a Roman laundry. Unaware of his gifts, he has no hope or protection from the greedy citizens and slaves who seek him out for sexual satisfaction. He resigns himself to his miserable fate with no money and no chance to earn his freedom. His luck changes when Longinus Megas, an enormously endowed Thracian slave, arrives at the laundry. He sees value in the handsome young slave. The much stronger Longinus defends and promotes Formosus, who easily accommodates the massive needs of his heroic protector. Many Roman citizens will part with money for a chance to be with these two extraordinary men. Together, they hatch a plan to gain their freedom.

THE SLAVES OF ROME

An Erotic Historical Romance

PETER SCHUTES

INTRODUCTION

Ancient Roman Society was arranged in a hierarchy with Patricians at the top, Plebeians in the middle, and Slaves at the bottom. In between were Freedmen, Soldiers, and Women. No matter where you were situated on the societal ladder, the slave was the lowest. A slave was owned. His owner had great freedom to use the slave as he saw fit. There were laws that protected slaves from sheer brutality, but they were difficult to enforce, for a slave was not permitted to use the legal system. Slaves could be loaned, borrowed, or sold. If a slave were ever set free, he could never be a citizen, but he could enjoy most of the rights of the Plebeians as a Freedman.

A delicate boy like our hero is likely to fall to the lowest rank in ancient society. He is not only a slave to his owner but to fellow slaves. His submissive nature leaves him vulnerable to the cruelty of the society around him. True love, a magical balm, seeks to right the imbalance and heal the scars that slavery has inflicted. Few in this world are lucky enough to find such love. Most remain scarred for life.

--Peter Schutes, 1959 Santa Monica, CA

FULLONICA

My name is Formosus Petro, and I was once a slave in Rome. In the winter before the locusts came, I lived with my family in a province East of Rome called Sabini. We were in a valley that had never been part of the Roman Empire. We didn't pay taxes, and we had our own language. It was during this cold winter that Rome appointed a governor to Sabini. With him came the Publicans and the army to collect tribute to the Emperor. We refused, and the army wiped out our whole valley, my parents included. Rome was cruel and vicious in its dealings with rebels, but they were merciful to children. I was plucked up by an ugly, fat Guard who auctioned me off to an even more hideous, fatter landlord named Porcius Pravus. I lost everything when I became a slave.

I grew from a boy to a man working for Porcius in his laundry, which Romans call a Fullonica. I was a fuller. Romans brought us their dirty togas. We laundered the togas with fine earth and urine, rinsing them four times, making them shine almost as brightly as when they were first woven. Porcius was not kind, but he was not cruel to children. It wasn't until my beard came in completely that he began mistreating me. By then, I had spent over ten years working for him. I had seen him mistreat other slaves, but I believed he wouldn't do that to me. He did.

The day it started, he sent Crassus Incommodus, his house slave, to summon me to his inner chambers. I hoped maybe he would release me from bondage, but it was quite the opposite. I entered the salon where Porcius reclined and ate meats, cheeses, and fruits. I eyed the plate of thinly sliced meat hungrily.

"Formosus, does the meat entice you?"

I nodded vigorously.

"You may have some of my meat, but first, you must do other things for me." Porcius removed his toga, then sat naked on the padded bench. "Come here, and I will show you." The things he did to me first were startling, but some were very pleasant. I enjoyed the enema and his tongue afterward on my clean hole. Like his fat body, his prick was thick and short. He asked me to place it in my mouth. He emphasized how important it was for me to wet it with saliva, as we did with stubborn stains in his Fullonica. I didn't know what difference it would make, but I obeyed his orders. I learned, in a most painful manner, why it was needed. Porcius had grown erect, which did nothing to increase the length of his short cock, but it was swollen to twice its thickness. He placed the dark red member at my rectum and pressed inward. I tried to scream, but he shoved a linen cloth into my mouth to quiet me. I cried and whimpered, but he continued to force his way into my anus.

That same night, as he rhythmically plunged his short fat cock into me, I made a discovery. It was not a terrible feeling after all. The pain was replaced with a pleasant pressure in my lower rectum. I was even more surprised when a clear liquid began to leak from my small hard penis. Later, when his cock spat hot white semen into me, I, too, shot ropes of my sperm on his toga and the divan.

This became a frequent event. Doing this service for Porcius was filled with pleasure, but the fact that I had no say or choice when or where to do it left me without a sense of self.

Crassus Incommodus, the house slave, saw my spirit broken. He was all too happy to take advantage of my troubled mind. He tripped me and whipped me, forced me to do for him what I did for his owner, accepting him inside me. His prick was a long, thick, spotted slab of meat. It smelled of rotten meat. He was far less gentle than Porcius when penetrating me. I couldn't relax enough; It hurt for weeks. I finally resisted and accepted my role in the laundry. Other fellow slaves wanted to relieve themselves in me, and I was too defeated to resist. I worked to the point of exhaustion, cleaning togas by day and getting rutted all night. Some of my coworkers would make an excuse to secret me away in an alley during the work day. At night, the line of takers was so long I couldn't possibly satisfy them all before bedtime. I often found myself dozing off with a slave humping me, then waking to find someone else inside me. I hated to admit how much I enjoyed the pleasurable sensations of being fucked. It made me ashamed. The little, short cocks hurt; I liked the one or two that were long enough to push past the inner sphincter and sufficiently thick to create pressure in my rectum and squeeze the fluid from me. Were it not for the love of sex, I am certain I would have chosen to end my own life. I was a worn sandal, filled by a different foot at all hours of the day. I had been proud once. Now, I only knew depravity and shame. Whatever made me who I am, it was stomped by that dirty sandal and crushed.

I suspected my station in life would never improve. My broken spirit surely caught the gods' attention; they sent me one of their own. Longinus Megas was a soldier from Thrace. Like me, his village resisted Rome, but unlike Sabini, no one was spared. Longinus was their fiercest warrior, having slain more than a dozen soldiers. He was the last survivor of his village. How he came to be at the Fullonica of Porcius Pravus is his story to tell.

He appeared one afternoon, bound and gagged. His tunic was stained with blood. When they released his gag, he didn't bite or spit. He appeared to have accepted his fate. Porcius asked Crassus to tend to his wounds, but Crassus had his own slave: me. He handed me a bottle of clean water, some mint salve, and a scrap of linen. "Go to the changing room and clean this vile piece of filth."

In the privacy of the changing room, we stood as I wiped away the blood from his lips. His eyes were a pale green, unlike anything I had ever seen. His dark brown curly hair was almost red. A light scattering of freckles graced his visage. He smiled at me as I dabbed at his lips.

"Do you speak the Roman tongue?" I asked.

"I do."

He had deep, terrifying wounds all up and down his back.

"Do you want me to put some on your lower back?"

The warrior nodded.

"I must unfasten your tunic."

"Of course."

I removed his tunic. He had whip wounds worse than any I had seen. They were going to scar his perfect, muscular body. The salve wouldn't be enough. I hoped he would forgive me.

He could not adjust his loincloth with his hands still tied behind his back. I gasped in horror when it came unraveled and fell to the ground.

"Sorry, oh, please forgive me."

"Relax, friend, just put it back."

As I bent to gather the cloth, my eye followed a long, fat, serpentine line of flesh to his knees.

I heard his laughter above me.

I smiled as I gathered up his manhood inside the cloth. "How do you prefer it tied?"

"Tight. It must hold a lot."

I nodded. "Yes, yes, it must."

I felt something strange in his presence. I believe it was his odor, but it may have been other humors that caused my heart to race. My face grew hot. He was very clever; he spotted my embarrassment immediately.

"Do you like what you see?"

I couldn't answer; I could only turn a darker shade of red.

"Relax, boy - what is your name?"

"Formosus Petro, formerly of Sabini."

"I'm Longinus Megas of Thrace." He clasped my wrist in greeting. I grabbed his wrist in return, although it was far too thick for my hand to encircle.

I kept stealing downward glances, ensuring my eyes hadn't deceived me. In his undergarment, there was still an abnormal gathering of flesh. I felt my own fill with blood, but it would not be noticed by anyone, for it was very small. Not more than a pollex.

Crassus burst in.

"Formosus, you've wasted far too much time. Come stomp in the orinari."

"But Crassus, I'm not finished. Look at his back."

Crassus smacked me so hard that I saw stars.

"His back is no concern of yours."

"Hey!" Longinus barked his fury at the evil little slave.

Crassus cowered.

"He told you he's not done!"

The wretched little man pointed at Longinus. "You are nobody. Silence." It came out weakly.

To complete his point, Longinus kicked the ground out from under Crassus. The slave got up and left us, muttering curses.

"You really don't want to make an enemy of him. He has the ear of the master."

"You mean Porky Pravus? I'm not going to be his slave for very long."

Crassus reappeared with a steaming hot pot of concentrated urine and wood ash. This was used to remove the dirt from clothes. It burned the skin, whether hot or cold.

Crassus spoke, "I can't burn your body, or the master will be very disappointed. But this little one, he is of no consequence." He held the pot above me. I struggled to break free. Longinus could do very little with his hands tied. His arm muscles bulged, and he snapped the ropes. Crassus wasn't ready for him. Longinus wrestled the pot from him and threw it in a corner, where it sizzled. He then held the ugly slave by his lapels.

"I only fight fair. To beat a weakling such as you in a fight, I might accidentally kill you. But know this, if you ever mistreat Formosus again, I won't hesitate to end your life with my own hands."

Crassus slithered away in false obeisance.

"There will be consequences," Longinus said, "but you are the first person to show me kindness since I was sold into bondage. That is why I choose to defend you. I also like the touch of your small, gentle hands."

I blushed yet again. "Nothing is worth having your beautiful skin destroyed. Your back may heal, but you will see and remember the signs of the whip until the grave."

Longinus smiled. "Sometimes, returning the kind actions of a friend is worth any sacrifice."

Now that I had time, I retrieved some Sabinian herbs from under my bed and boiled them. To the herbal brew, I added Fuller's Earth. Longinus watched thoughtfully as I prepared the poultice. I took strips of linen and coated them in the mud. I laid them down along the lines of the whip, just as I had seen my mother do for father when he cut himself on the plow. The strips had to be long enough to go from his back over his massive shoulder to the front, where I could attach them to his stomach ripples. When these were laid, I wound him in dry linen around the midsection to hold everything in place.

As I patted each piece of linen smooth, I saw him adjust the frighteningly large penis trapped in his loincloth. Soft its length was over a palmus major. I am sure it would exceed a pes when erect. He wanted to put it in me, I knew. I wasn't sure I could manage something so huge. I bent down to allow him to lift my tunic and examine my bottom. He didn't touch me. His rejection brought tears.

"Hey, what's wrong?" Longinus held my chin and looked into my troubled eyes.

"You do not desire me."

"You made it a declaration," he said, "not a question. Try again."

"Do you desire me?"

Longinus ran his tongue along his lips and lifted my tunic. He inspected the front and the back.

"In different circumstances, I would say 'yes.' But we are slaves. We don't get to indulge our desires."

I shook my head and smiled. "You haven't been a fuller for but a few hours. You would be surprised what happens when no one is looking."

The giant snake living in Longinus's loincloth must have reared its head; the loincloth fell again.

"Formosus, you are devious. See how your mere words cause my undergarment to fall?"

I nodded. He bent to pick it back up.

"Now that your big hands are freed from the ropes, you may want to use them to hold my hips." I bent and presented my hole. "Everyone else does it."

In my constant dalliances with the slaves, I discovered that the melted fat of a pig, when inserted into my rectum, made all my encounters less painful. Since my suitors were constant and without warning, I had to prepare. I washed my bottom every morning and used a small bladder to clean the inside, as Porcius taught me. I then applied the pig grease to my insides. In the afternoon, I applied more after a quick enema. With the addition of saliva, the pain usually disappeared. Longinus didn't know this. The warrior's incredible cock was rising to full attention. I thought it huge when it was asleep. As it grew, it was even bigger and thicker, like a stallion. It may have been a cubit. He shook his head.

"We need to prepare. Even then, you're a small fellow, and I think I might split you in two. It's happened before."

I smiled and took the head of his cock. I coated it with saliva and then placed it at the entrance to my anus. I pushed back. Longinus's head was the size of an apple. My hole was not prepared. The pain reminded me of the first day with Porcius. I wanted to scream but kept my pain from escaping. I let out a soft moan instead of a cry of agony. I passed a significant milestone; Longinus' head was entirely inside me.

"Formosus, are you sure you want to do this?" The concern in his voice told a long, sad story. I think he may have asked the same question to others and received a negative response. I was good at one thing more than any other. It was time to prove it. In answer, I pushed my rear closer to him, feeling the head and equally thick shaft work their way to a wall deep inside me. I didn't know that wall existed. No one at the Fullonica had ever gone deep enough to reach this spot. I looked back, expecting him to be buried, but it was only half. I didn't know how to continue.

"Twist to your left." He commanded.

I did as I was told and felt the head make its way around a corner and into my belly. I'm naturally thin, but on a slave's diet, I am skin and bones. My abdomen rippled and bulged as the massive cock pushed deeper inside me. I had my back to Longinus so that he couldn't see. There would be time for shifting positions later. My first order of business was to feel Longinus's hips press against my flat, skinny bottom. At last, they did. He was buried all the way.

Just as I had imagined, Longinus was a talented lover. He held my hips and plunged in and out of me. He was buried so deep I could have taken several steps, and he would have still been inside me. There was none of the little-cock-popping-out problems. Even though I felt pain the entire length of his travels, it was eclipsed by the pleasures he imparted.

"Longinus, you're perfect." I don't know if he understood what I meant. His penis, and the body it was attached to, were the perfect match for me. I reached behind and put my little hands on his big muscular ass. He groaned with delight.

"Formosus, you're beautiful."

The pressure in my rectum, ten times normal, caused a massive river of clear fluid to pour out of me. I caught most of it in my hand. Longinus held my wrist, brought the penis broth to his lips, and then drank. Nobody had ever done that with me. He then grabbed my neck and placed his lips on mine. His tongue, and a great deal of salty fluid, filled my mouth. Our lips touching like this caused more fluid to puddle on the floor below me.

I wanted to be even closer to Longinus. He sensed my need and lifted me, twisting me around on his colossal skewer of flesh. He set me softly on the changing bench. We faced one another now. My heels rested on his shoulders. His muscled arms held him above the bench.

I traced my hand across the head of his penis as it

passed along my belly. His eyes bulged when he saw his cock tracing lines across my abdomen.

"Is that me?"

"Yes. You're the first ever to go there."

My compliment had a powerful effect. He pulled out very far, then plunged in all the way. The pace grew faster. I had been penetrated hard and fast but never by one so enormous. His thick cock was pressing in new places, which caused me distress. I was sure my bladder would burst from the beating it was getting. I tried desperately, then, to my shame, I spilled urine all over my belly, splashing it onto Longinus.

"Did I just fuck the piss out of you?"

I nodded, ashamed of my incontinence.

"You make me feel so powerful, Formosus. I can make you pee." He surprised me by licking my lips before pressing his tongue into my mouth. He pounded more, and I urinated down his legs. The cock bulge protruding from my abdomen moved faster, then suddenly slowed.

He was giving off signs that I knew well; he was going to come.

I wrapped my hands around my belly skin to trap his cock head. I squeezed and rubbed up and down the top of his cock. It was like hand-fishing for eels. His eyes were like gold chargers. He couldn't believe I could do such a thing.

"Formosus, I'm close."

"I know." I smiled.

Longinus put his hand on my little penis and rubbed it with his rough palm. I arched my back; the pleasure was intense. My tiny penis was sensitive. Only once or twice in my years of sexual servitude had I been touched there. My pleasure was nobody's concern. Longinus felt otherwise.

"Your penis is so perfect." He said. I laughed out loud. Pulling halfway out, he stooped and took my nipple-sized penis in his mouth. I would much rather he be buried deep, so I lifted his head and used my feet to pull his butt closer to me. His sweat trickled onto my body. It smelled of my poultice and his manliness. I lifted a drop to my nostril and inhaled the musky scent. It reminded me that his cock filled my lower body with its fleshy girth. Oh, that sent me over the edge.

My tiny erection reared up and spit out a colossal load of white cum. Longinus reached a finger and coated it with my cream. When he put it in his mouth, he gasped.

"Oh shit, Formosus. I'm coming! I'm -- aargh!" He was so deeply embedded in me that I couldn't feel the semen. Maybe he had torn me open and was coming on my heart! He threw his head back. He scooped up more of my semen and ate it, then leaned forward and kissed me, transferring some of my own seed into my mouth.

After his orgasm, Longinus leaned on my body and panted. He remained deep inside me until he grew soft. My body ejected him in a slow, slithering exit. The suction caused by his massive cock head dragged his load of semen with it. The journey was long. After many minutes of exquisite pleasure, the head popped out. He was prepared; he held out his hand and caught the fruits of his exertion in his cupped palm until it was full. The rest had nowhere to go. It drained onto the floor in a continuous stream. He held his cupped palm full of semen to my mouth and urged me to drink. I took a sip and felt my whole body spasm. It was so full of male essence, it gave me a rush of pleasure. I took another small sip. I felt muscles growing just from the flavor. He took a sip and smiled.

"You need the rest, Formosus. It will make you stronger." Longinus held his broad, hairy hand out and forced me to swallow the remainder of his essence. He was right; I could feel myself gaining strength as I lay on the bench, dripping his thick semen from my sloppy, stretched asshole.

Later that day, Porcius had Longinus flogged again for his insolence while defending me. It undid any of the kindness I might have shown him. I felt terrible.

RED HOT POKER

In the evening hours, Longinus lay next to me in my stall on the hay-strewn floor. I had kept the herbal mud moist and used it again to soothe his new torn flesh. Longinus established dominance in the hierarchy. Even as his back dripped with blood, he silently declared me his property. Slaves who had been free to grab me and use me for their pleasure were afraid to come near. The warrior protected me. Not even Crassus Commodus, with his jangling ring of keys, could get to me for his pleasure. He and a few others paced near my stall - *our* stall - and grumbled. At first, when I was denied the pleasure of more sex, I felt desperate. But remembering Longinus and his masterful prick, I was able to quiet the hunger for cock.

"What do they want?"

I didn't want to put it into words. I placed Longinus's hand on my rear, pressing one of his fingers into the loose crack.

"I imagine they've never had finer."

It was not the response I expected. He wasn't disgusted, and he wasn't ashamed of me. "You do? I'm a slave and a whore. What do you see in me?"

"I see an incredible blond boy with a kind spirit shining from his sky-blue eyes."

I stopped applying the poultice. Nobody had said anything so kind since my village was slaughtered. I couldn't say anything; I was so scared. At last, after minutes of silence, I said, "And I see a handsome protective warrior with enormous strength and a fire smoldering behind his olive-green eyes." It was met with a loud snore.

Early in the morning, my warrior awoke in agony. Again, I applied the mud to the lashes on his back. I wanted to keep him thinking about other things. Distraction got me through the pain of pleasuring others.; I hoped it would work for Longinus.

"Tell me about how you know the Roman tongue."

"Oh, ouch. Yes, well, in Thrace, there are many schools. The children are taught numbers and letters, then how to read. Because Romans seem to own everything these days, the school taught us how to speak. Nobody at my school knew written Roman. But as you can tell, I know how to speak very well."

"You certainly do. You're smart, strong, and very handsome. You shouldn't be a slave working in a laundry. Were you betrothed?"

"No. I was not the kind of person to marry."

He looked over his shoulder at me to see my reaction. I smiled. "Me neither."

Longinus had questions for me. "Why do you let the other slaves have relations with you?"

"I have no choice."

"So, you don't like it?" Was that disappointment in his voice?

"I didn't say that. I would like to have a say in the matter. Instead, because I am weak, small, and pretty, they use me whenever and however they want."

"Do you like being used?" He wasn't just asking about the others. He wanted to be sure I wanted to be with him.

"That's hard to answer. I like the pleasurable feelings when I am with someone skilled enough to give them. I don't like the spit, the slaps, the punches, and the rape."

Longinus nodded. "Of course not. How terrible and cruel."

I added, "Done skillfully, it can be the best feeling in the world. At least I discovered that yesterday." I ran a finger across his muscled chest.

"Had you never been shown true pleasure?" He seemed horrified.

"I'd imagined it was pleasure, but you've shown me it was something much less."

The warrior said softly, "You don't have to imagine now. I can show you again and again."

I would have hugged him if his back weren't a crisscross of wounds. He continued, "I can take you to far-off lands, and you'll never leave your bed."

It was so early; the light wasn't up, and the cock hadn't crowed. I took a risk.

"Take me there now."

He rolled to face me, careful to avoid his back. He whispered, "Do you like being with a man who's really big down there?" He grabbed his crotch for emphasis

"I like it huge."

"You have excellent taste."

The slaves kept the crock of melted pig fat in my stall for their convenience. It was an insult that they thought I should smell like a pig. But, of course, it was extremely effective at smoothing out the roughness of intercourse, so it was practical.

I reapplied the stinky cream in and around my anus, then gave it to Longinus. He handed it back.

"I want you to do it for me."

He lifted his tunic. His loincloth was bursting at the seams. I unfastened a clasp, and his massive tree trunk sprung free, striking me in the belly. He wasn't even close to me!

I applied grease, frequently dipping into the pot. "I'm going to run out," I joked.

He smiled wistfully. Something has still not been said. He fumbled with my loincloth and watched as it fell away, revealing my tiny penis; His eyes lit up with delight.

"I love the small ones the best of all." I didn't think I should feel pride, but I did.

Then Longinus did something completely brand new. He grabbed my legs and hauled my backside up to his mouth. He created a continuous stream of saliva and spat it down my ass crack. My hole was stretched out. It resembled a vagina, with lips protruding. He had no trouble filling my anus with his saliva.

"This is going to make it easier." Longinus beamed. We lay on our side.

I knew it would be easy because he had stretched me. At least, that's how it was with everyone else. I was accustomed to their shape.

When his big red apple pushed against my crack, I smiled and wriggled back toward him.

The huge head didn't pop right in. It hurt. I was shocked. I was sore inside, everywhere. My whole world turned dark. Was I going to endure terrible pain from now on? Wouldn't that be worse than being a whore?

"It's going to hurt more today, at first." Longinus knew the effect his cock had on men's insides.

"But it will get better. By tomorrow, I promise it won't hurt at all. If we do it every day from then on, you'll feel no pain." I hoped he was right.

"It doesn't hurt." I lied. "I think we were made for each other."

I regretted saying that.

"Really?" Longinus pushed his way further inside me and kissed my neck. It felt like a red-hot poker was tearing me in two.

"Yes, Really. It feels great." A sex slave to slaves, I

was an accomplished liar. I didn't even let out the shriek of pain that was lurking just beneath those words. Longinus snaked his way around the corner and deep into my tummy. Everywhere his cock touched me, which was pretty much everywhere, I felt burning.

"Still good?" I was tempted to say 'no' to put an end to his fiery anal assault. But the smell of his sweat and the taste of his semen were powerful incentives.

"Good? No. It's great." I hoped I wouldn't regret that lie.

He pulled partway out, then back in slowly. It burned and stung.

"Oh, Formosus, I only ever dreamed I would find someone so perfect." I liked his compliment. Before I had time to protest, he started to move at a feverish jackrabbit pace, sliding easily, thanks to the saliva and pig fat. And a miracle happened; the pain decreased, then went away completely. Instead, it became a sneeze. It became a yawn. It became a good shit. It became a piss after holding it for two hours. It was every pleasurable body feeling you could think of. I didn't even know I had leaked fluid until Longinus put a salty finger in my mouth.

"Longinus, you're killing me with delight. I don't know how else to explain it."

"Don't say killing." He got very serious for a second. "Is it like being tickled?"

"Yes, and sneezing and peeing and many other enjoyable feelings."

Longinus smiled. "You're having an anal orgasm."

He was right. My body quivered with joy. I couldn't stop quaking. I pissed myself again.

"What did you do to me?" I asked the hulking man plunging deep inside me.

"I turned your ass into a vagina." When he said that, I wanted to be hurt or angry, but I could only feel the truth of my deep, deep vaginal ass. The sensations doubled and redoubled. My penis felt wet. I looked, and it was sitting in a large puddle of fluids. Longinus continuously kept up the rapid pace, driving me to a full-body orgasm. Every inch of my skin was alive with pleasure. I went blind. I couldn't see anything because my body was all feeling. I put my hand on my tummy and felt the hard fast pumping inside me. Because I touched myself right where Longinus was touching me deep inside, I had another seizure of excitement. I could feel Longinus in a spoon behind me. His breath blew against my neck, another pleasure spot.

I felt his hand cover my penis and rub it. "I'm coming soon."

The most sensitive spot on my already charged body, I nearly exploded when he rubbed me. Despite his vast muscles, his rough fucking, and his giant hand, he touched my penis with remarkable tenderness. It made me race toward orgasm. I tried to lift his hand away by the wrist, but he grunted like a pig.

"I'm touching you there. Don't fight it." He wasn't mean; he was just very forceful.

"I'm about to cum," I warned him.

"Meeeee toooo. Oh shit!"

Because my entire body was sensitive now, I felt load after load of hot cream pump out of his massive balls and up his shaft. I felt a small pond of come fill up my innards.

Because this man had entered my life and given me joy again after years of misery, I instantly felt a deep attachment to him. I think he felt the same for me. But now that he was flooding my insides with his semen, and I could feel it, I had another body spasm. His huge gentle hand rubbed me into ejaculation. I shot sperm on his fingers, the floor, and my chest. I heard him lick his fingers behind me. I also heard a dish being placed under my ass.

I looked over my shoulder and saw a clay bowl

poised to catch the warrior's sperm as it poured out of my ass. I turned my head behind me, and he leaned to kiss me. Our lips and tongues explored the other. I tasted my cum on his breath.

After ten minutes, his cock softened enough to begin the long, twisted journey out of me. The sheer length of his tool meant that pooping him out would take another ten minutes. I was in no hurry. I still had the occasional spasm as I felt the thickest part of his dick press on a fold or a sphincter. It was my boy-pussy reacting to being stretched.

At last, the apple-sized cockhead plopped out, narrowly missing the bowl. Next came the white flood of sperm. Drops at first, then rivulets, then a mighty flowing river of cum poured out of me into the clay bowl.

I heard Longinus curse. "Damn!"

"What is it, Long?"

"The bowl wasn't big enough." He cursed again.

"I'll clean it."

He was serious. "It's plenty. I want you to drink the whole bowl. You're going to need your strength." I began slurping the steamy load of sperm.

"My strength indeed," I said, "I thought you were going to fuck me to death."

"Don't say that!" He was crazed. I thought he would hit me.

"I'm sorry." He could hear the tears in my voice.

"Listen, Formosus, I owe you an explanation, so remember to ask me."

I was gulping down the last hot mouthfuls of come from the bowl. "Explanation for what? Strength or Death?"

"Both."

✳ 3 ✳

PISSPOTS

We held on to one another until it was time to report to the laundry. Once we were dressed and present, Crassus gave the worst job to Longinus. He would put the filthy clothes into the Orinari, filled with piss, and stomp them until they were thoroughly soaked with the malodorous brew. They were transferred to a long table where several slaves brushed the fabric with fuller's earth. A series of 4 rinses in clear running water brought the garments to the most senior slaves, who worked in pairs to wring out the fabric and hang it out to dry in the courtyard of Porcius. Crassus had the enviable job of folding the dry garments. It could be done in an hour or two.

Because I was bottom-most on the social hierarchy, they gave me the next worst task of replenishing the Orinari. This entailed running back and forth to a dozen corners, swapping full piss pots for empty ones. We provided buckets where men pissed, providing us with our most potent detergent. I could carry four buckets at a time if they were not overflowing. I replaced each full pisspot with a clean one. I returned to the fullonica with four filled buckets, then spent time in the Orinari, stomping togas next to Longinus.

There was much humiliation with this job. More

than once, urinating men in the streets had asked me to clean the urine from the tip of their foreskin using my mouth. Whether or not I agreed, we would retire to a dark alley or dead-end. There, the man would force me to bring him to completion in my throat.

Although none of the urinators were as impressive as my new protector, some were very well endowed. That is how I learned to pleasure men in this way without vomiting. Dozens of men who demanded my oral skills were long enough to pass the back of my throat and continue down my esophagus. It was meant to be degrading, forcing a slave to eat your semen. Secretly, it was a pleasure for me. I wondered how Longinus would feel if he saw me doing this service so willingly.

The urinators I detested were those who wanted to use me as a bucket. They roughly forced my mouth open, sometimes right on the street with passersby, and emptied themselves all over me. One beast would give me a beating if I didn't drink his "yellow wine," as he called it. Because I also stomped in the Orinari, nobody ever questioned why I came back soaked in piss.

Life could improve. I needed to decide between enduring this piss-drinking humiliation, along with the pleasure of receiving semen from dozens of penises, or asking for Longinus to protect me. He would never let this or any other kind of indignity befall me if he knew about it. That would mean my sex life, already severely diminished in the slave quarters, would surely end in the streets. I lived for so long without the respect of my fellow man that it felt empty to imagine a life without humiliation.

Today, my favorite Legionary, Claudius, was relieving himself in a long golden arc. The source of the yellow stream was not thick but very long. He caught me watching and smiled.

"Just a minute, love. I've held it since last night."

I shrugged and smiled politely. Slaves were prohibited from speaking to Legionaries unless posing or answering a question.

Claudius shook himself roughly, releasing most of the urine but not all.

"Here's our chance, Boy. Let's retire to the alley so you can get me nice and clean. I don't want any piss in my loincloth. And there's so much plumbing; I can never get it all out."

"Formosus."

"I beg your pardon?"

"I am called Formosus."

My words hung in the air, unanswered for far too long. Claudius had every right to beat me. I spoke out of turn.

But the corners of his mouth turned up, and he let out a hearty laugh.

"I don't need to know your name, Boy. You're not a citizen. A slave."

His laughter hurt, and he saw. He rubbed a rough palm across my lips. Would he slap me?

"You weren't born a slave, were you?"

"No more than you were born a Legionary."

He put his arm around my neck. "Here we are. This is dark enough." He pulled my skull towards his hardening cock head. In one continuous motion, I inhaled his thin prick and took him past my throat into the esophagus. I didn't gag.

"Oh, you are a talented one...Formosus. Where did you learn that trick?"

With my mouth full, I could only gesture to the surrounding alley. He bellowed with laughter. I could have pointed at him. I had done this a hundred times with him. He was one of the longest, so it was with him I learned to go very deep. But he didn't know me. I could be any slave in the street.

"I'm playing with you, boy. Formosus. Do you think

I don't remember teaching you that trick myself? You're the best cocksucker in Rome."

I took a breath and replanted my lips in his pubic hairs. He knew me, and now he knew my name. Slaves have no name. I was never so bold and aggressive. With Longinus as a protector and his bowl of sperm in my belly, I felt confidence I hadn't known since my en-slavement.

With a gentle rocking motion, I slid Claudius in and out of my food chute, breathing quickly when needed. The gentle rubbing of his cock against my tonsils awoke that all-over body sneeze. Each time his long penis rubbed against my throat, it felt like an orgasm. He was too deep into his own pleasant sensations to notice my spasms.

Claudius held my skull still and fucked my mouth like a pussy. I put my hand on my throat below the Adam's apple. He was surprised when I squeezed, giving his head a narrow passage. I didn't do it for him. The added friction intensified my waves of lust.

"Oh, little man, you learned well." He picked up speed until he was pounding so hard his balls smacked my chin.

I had work to do, so I hurried things along. I put a finger in Claudius's rear. It worked.

"Ah, Formosus, you sly devil! I'm going to, uh, uh, I'm going to come!"

And he did. He hurriedly pulled his cock from my mouth and painted my face white with his Legionary sperm. He put the head back in my mouth for me to finish the cleaning.

"That's it, boy. Just make it nice and clean. Good boy." He pulled the whole length away from me and curled it up like a sleeping serpent in his loincloth. He tossed a Quadrans at me, but my eyes were filled with his semen, which burned. I couldn't see to catch. I lifted my toga, wiping his seed from my face. He chuckled.

"Oh, Formosus. You didn't get much when the gods bestowed dick."

I knew my small penis made me more attractive to most men, but it hurt coming from Claudius. I resisted the urge to ask who the aggressor would be were mine large like his. Insolence would destroy our tense friendship.

By the time I found the coin, Claudius was gone.

I collected four full pots of urine and hurried back to the fullonica.

Longinus made a terrible face when I dumped four buckets of urine into the Orinari. His great size helped when stomping the garments. I joined him in the Orinari. I stamped and waited for my next outing to start. I usually stomped for a short time before collecting more buckets. If I wasted too much time, I might find the buckets overflowing. If Porcius were levied a fine by the vigiles, he would throttle me.

I talked to Longinus about the bucket brigade.

"Yes, so I can only carry four full buckets at a time. If I'm quick, six buckets will just contain sufficient urine to fill four empties."

Longinus nodded. "Would eight buckets be enough to empty all twelve?"

I nodded. "Probably. Too bad I have but two arms."

"You shall have four arms on this next excursion." He pointed at Gaius, a fat nervous slave, and snapped his fingers. "Hey, you! Get over here. You're taking over."

Just like that, Longinus rearranged the work detail. Crassus was lazy; he rarely visited the Orinari. Gaius hopped from leg to leg, unhappy with his new assignment.

We talked as we walked to the corners I hadn't yet visited today.

"This job, Formosus, is it gratifying? You are the only one who leaves the shop and sees the streets."

"It's freedom. Even though the job is the lowest status, it's the best. I never tell anyone. They all think I am being punished."

Longinus smiled. "Do you run into any trouble?"

"Oh, there are some awful men who force me to drink their piss. Otherwise, it's not bad."

I heard bones crack in Longinus's fists. "Show me these men, and I will guarantee your safety from now on."

I shivered with desire. Having a protector was a great joy. I didn't tell him about the men who used my throat. I didn't want that to end.

At the third stop, a cruel Publican grabbed my hair and forced me to my knees to take his piss in plain sight of everyone.

"Open it! You know what..."

He never got to finish his sentence. He lay on his back. Longinus pressed a urine-soaked sandal to his throat.

"Open wide." Longinus didn't wait for the Publican; he just unleashed a powerful stream of urine on the man's face. The man shrieked, but Longinus kept going until he was empty. He let his dong swing from leg to leg.

"He's mine. Any more bullshit, and you'll wish I only pissed on you."

I felt my miniature manhood grow hard under my tunic. Longinus turned and winked as the Publican ran away.

A small crowd had gathered when Longinus pulled out his pecker. It was all men. A red-haired slave couldn't help himself.

"Please, sir, may I touch it?"

"I cannot charge you money, so be quick."

The redhead held it, caressed it, kissed it, then scurried away. Longinus fastened his loincloth tightly to bind the massive meat once more.

A wealthy politician stepped forward.

"I can pay you. Are you interested?"

Longinus grinned. "What did you have in mind?"

"I want to watch your slave give you oral service."

Longinus cast a glance at me. "Can you?"

I shook my head. I knew I could take him in my anus, but my small mouth and throat had never been plugged and stretched by such a giant.

The politician walked away, but Longinus brought him back. "Sir, how much would you pay if he takes me all the way?"

The politician smiled. "That is worth a denarius."

"And just the head?"

"I would offer one As for just the foreportion."

"If he struggles but cannot?"

"It merits a Quadrans, but he must struggle for much time."

The three of us retreated to a dead end. The accumulated trash told us this street was never used. Longinus once more unleashed his manhood, letting the loincloth fall to his side.

I was quite doubtful that I could manage this. I could barely touch together two hands when he was erect. He was soft now. There was some hope.

I knelt before my protector and placed the giant soft head against my lips. I was exciting him, and he was growing. I had to act quickly. Using all the lessons my legionary friend Claudius had taught me and wishing there were lessons to manage the dreadful girth, I slipped the head into my mouth. The first gate was crossed. We had already earned one As. My lips would only stretch so far. I felt the skin crack at the edges of my mouth.

"Oh my." The politician wiped sweat from his brow and played with his penis under his gold-trimmed toga.

Longinus was not done growing, but he was hard enough to allow me to push his swelling cockhead to the back of my throat. I wasn't quick enough. The head had doubled in size and stayed lodged between my tonsils. I felt the corners of my mouth rip further as the flesh doubled in size.

"Oh, Formosus, you are the first!" I glanced upward to see Longinus beaming down at me. Oh, how I wanted to please him! He had taken the whip for me. I could suffer for him.

I welled up with pride. Claudius had taught me to extract saliva from the cheeks and mucus from the nose, moving it to the back of my throat. That provides a slick surface to help the cock slide past the tonsils into the deeper throat.

Sniffing and squeezing enough mouth fluids to make a difference took time. I tried many times to force him past. Just when the politician was ready to call it off, I had a breakthrough. The gigantic log of flesh penetrated my esophagus. With pain and relief, I forced myself towards Longinus's hairy root until nothing was left exposed. I had him entirely inside me.

Longinus thrust back and forth, further loosening my throat muscles. With a panic, I realized that I would have to pull him out of there so I could breathe. I allowed him to deeply fuck my throat until I couldn't stand another second without air. I pulled back and panicked. The corona of his penis was the thickest part. He was jammed in my throat.

"Formosus?" Whatever choking looked like, it was enough to scare Longinus. He yanked hard, and the head flew out of my mouth. I caught my breath, then pushed him deep inside again until my nose was once more buried in his crotch.

I felt drops of hot liquid on my arm. The politician had orgasmed. It didn't stop him. He kept going. I discovered how to yank Longinus back to my tonsils to allow me to breathe. Once I had the timing, I gave Longinus lots of time deep inside me. I also took a few breaks by rubbing the slippery shaft with both my hands while I slurped his generous supply of pre-come from the head.

After a long time fucking me hard and deep near my stomach, I heard a beautiful sound.

"Oh, shit." Two better words cannot be heard when sucking cock in the streets.

I reared back, exposing his whole stiff cock. Seeing it in its full glory, I marveled that I could have swallowed the head, let alone the massive shaft. He extended a thick, muscled arm and grabbed his manhood in his meaty, hairy hand.

"Open up."

I obeyed. He quickly jerked himself to the precipice.

"Fuck, Formosus. Oh, God. Ohhhh!" And he shot a small batch of semen on my face and tongue. He then fired a torrent of cum directly into my mouth, hitting the back of my throat. I swallowed it with my mouth open. As new floods came, I couldn't keep up. Soon, my mouth was a waterfall of white-hot semen, wasted on the ground.

Again, I felt spatters and saw the politician firing rounds in the air, hitting me, Longinus, and some nearby pigeons.

"Bravo! Sophos!" The politician clapped his come-drenched hands.

We continued our rounds, gathering buckets of piss, one denarius richer.

ADVERTISEMENT

Longinus's mighty cock swung broadly under his tunic. Longinus had left his loincloth at the dead end, so we reversed our journey to retrieve it. Plebeians and Nobiles alike took notice of the powerful prize that peeked out from time to time. I overheard a wife say to her upper-class husband, "My next gift should look like that."

The nobleman wiped his brow. His face wore a mixture of desire, shame, envy, and fear. It was 832 ad urbes. He needn't be ashamed. He lived in the largest, most progressive city in the world. Longinus flashed the husband a winning smile, and they both swooned. A pang of jealousy stabbed my heart. He was mine. They could watch a show, but—

"Excuse me. Whose slave are you?"

Longinus held four buckets high. I mimicked him.

"Oh, you're two of Porcius Pravus's fullones. I pity you both. I'm sorry to keep you waiting with your, uh, arms full, but my wife pointed out a tremendous blessing bestowed upon you by the gods."

We set our buckets down. Longinus toyed with the man. "Which of us are you talking about? It must be Formosus, with his perfect bottom." He playfully lifted my tunic and displayed my smooth, soft rump to the Nobiles. The husband was quiet while his wife spoke.

"That is indeed a blessing, but not the one of which we speak."

Longinus squeezed my cheeks to force my mouth open. "Is it this cavernous hole that can only be filled by someone...with my prowess?"

The wife blurted to Longinus, "Not the hole but the snake, dear."

Longinus beamed, then lifted his tunic. The husband gasped, and his wife shrieked in terror.

"I take it back. I don't want such a massive gift."

Longinus turned to the husband, his tunic still lifted high. "And you, sir."

The Nobilis ran his hand through his grey beard.

"What a marvel. Jove be praised; you were granted great mercies."

I thought this was the end of our conversation, but Longinus knew otherwise.

"Many find it titillating to watch a performance. A carnal comedy with a happy ending."

The couple, who had been married since the previous century, turned and silently spoke to one another with nods and smiles.

"How much are tickets to such an event? It defies the imagination that anyone can survive such a beast."

Longinus winced at the words. For a fleeting instant, I saw his lip curl into a snarl; then, he grinned broadly as he continued his sales pitch.

"Colossal though it may be, it is often best enjoyed in a more private setting."

The husband was not interested in a protracted discussion.

"I can pay you five denarii for a private performance in our villa. The Villa Saturnus. Do you know it?" I nodded.

Longinus knew the depth of the pockets on this

man. "This performance is a gift for your wife. Do you only value her a mere five denarii? She is more valuable than silver, for she is gold. For the price of one Aureus, you will have a performance that shall remain emblazoned in your happiest of memories."

The man's wife glared at him. He nodded. One Aureus.

Longinus laid down rules as though he had always known them. "That Aureus is for a private performance. If you wish to bring an orgy of your friends to dazzle, we require an additional five denarii per person. Much like admission to the Colosseum. But the colossus will be so much closer, in the flesh."

The Nobilis spoke. "It may take some time to arrange. I am well acquainted with your master. He will tell you when to come to the villa."

We found the missing loincloth atop a pile of rotting African fruit. It was lucky we worked in a fullonica. He wrapped the filthy cloth around a bucket handle and went untethered for our rounds. With so much meat swinging beneath his tunic, Longinus was a walking billboard for his "gift." We were already booked for a performance with the Saturni. Longinus refused all askers, making us seem all the more valuable to the greedy nobility.

❧ 5 ❧

DICK OF DEATH

O ur arms were full of piss buckets, so I could not show him my obeisance and servitude. He was my master, not Porcius. Words would have to suffice.

"It is an exquisite pleasure to work with you, Longinus."

"Did you like taking me in the mouth? You are the first, you know. The gods blessed you in unimaginable ways."

"It was difficult at first. I feared you might kill me or tear my throat apart." Longinus should have laughed but instead came to a sudden stop.

"What is it? Do you miss your mother and father?" I was shocked to see tears in his eyes. He shook his head.

"Formosus, were you ever singled out by other children because you were different down there?"

I cringed. "I dread recalling the terrible names. Mouse meat. Thumb-dick. Penis minima."

Longinus added, "Such names exist for me too."

"But surely they are spoken with pride!"

Longinus shook his head. "They are ugly, too."

"What is uglier than 'mouse meat'?"

"Shit collector." I winced. That was ugly.

I asked, "You know they say these things to you out of envy, don't you?"

He smiled, "It may be the same for you, Formosus."

"Really? Only catamites and lady-boys wish for such a small endowment. I would give anything to have your powerful cock. I have wanted a bigger penis since childhood, more than anything else in the world."

Longinus shrugged. "My cock is yours. You shall have it every night."

"That isn't the same!"

He grew mischievous, "Not the same, no. I'm told it is much better. By the sounds you make, I know it must be true."

"We have strayed, Longinus. What do these names and jealousies have to do with your tears?"

He grew melancholy again. His story began. "The name that hurt me most and still does to this day was Thanatophallus. It means 'dick of death' in Western Thrace."

"That doesn't sound as nasty as 'shit collector.'"

We arrived at the fullones. Nearly three hours had passed, and the Orinari was dry. Crassus would hear about it from the many abusers in my midst. I would get a beating like Longinus.

Eight full buckets nearly made up for it. Together, Longinus and I stomped in a much deeper pool of urine now. The backed-up robes and garments moved through quickly to the mud rinse. Together, we were strong.

While we marched in place, Longinus continued his story.

"In my village, there was a beautiful girl named Elena. Her blue eyes and blonde hair set her apart from the other girls. She came from a noble family, and I was a farmer's son, so there was no chance we could be together. I badly yearned for enough gold to buy my nobility, but we were poor. Elena forever gave me longing looks, and we both knew we wanted each other."

I felt myself seize up with jealousy over this unknown girl.

He continued. "After she married a rich, overweight slob, he took her maidenhead. This meant, at last, we could indulge our desires, and no one would know. I planned our first dalliance in the barn where my father kept his sheep. On a bed of straw, we lay together, letting our lips explore each other's skin. Elena was everything I ever wanted...at that moment."

I was relieved he added the extra disclaimer. I could never be Elena, after all.

"She was experienced now, and I still a beginner, so she took the lead. She removed my tunic and frowned at my loincloth. I never expected a frown. So many schoolmates had envied and praised me when they jerked me to orgasm. Why did she tremble?"

I knew why.

"When she couldn't bring herself to reveal my penis, I untied and dropped my undergarment. I expected delight but only saw terror. I asked if she wished to continue."

"And did she?" I wasn't sure where his story would go.

He hung his head and trembled. "Yes."

Suddenly, I knew the direction, if not the ending.

"We had waited since childhood to fuck; we were anxious to make the other happy. I was a virgin with no technique. I rutted her like a stable horse. Her cries and moans spurred me on further, harder, faster. Her moans became sobs. At one point, she begged me to stop. When I asked if she was sure, I got no answer. She quietly endured my inexpert fucking. Unaware of the strength of my member, I hammered five minutes longer until, at last, I unleashed a flood of semen that filled her like a cup. When I removed my cock from her, it was red with blood.

"I tried to revive Elena, but she would not awaken. Her breaths were shallow. The straw beneath her was red with blood and white with come. The red overtook the white as it poured from inside. I begged the gods for mercy. I had meant her no harm. She was the love of my life.

"She died in my arms. Were it not for the sudden invasion of Athenians, I would have surrendered to the executioner, for life was no longer endurable without the hope we could someday be together".

"You were invaded by Greeks?"

"Yes, they plundered, raped, and pillaged. Every able-bodied male between eighteen and fifty was conscripted into military duty. So many women were raped and killed that night; only the gods ever accused me of any wrongdoing. But the shame and remorse never went away."

My feet burned in the urine vat.

"So that is why you grimace if I mention anything dangerous or deadly about your prick. I'm very sorry."

"Yes, but that is only half the tale. It can wait for another time. Please, you must tell me how you are so talented in the art of giving men pleasure." Longinus grinned at me expectantly.

I started with the first time, with Porcius. "He cannot claim but a fraction of your length, but he competes with you in girth. He was my first, and I bled a lot. But each time he summoned me, it grew easier to tolerate."

"How did you come to be a sex slave to other slaves?"

"It happened naturally. Crassus was the first. His penis was so ugly I couldn't look at it. But it felt terrific once it was hidden away inside me. With my back to him, I was vulnerable. Others saw and wanted my young bottom for their cocks. Soon, I experienced many shapes and sizes in my rectum. Most were small, though none so small as me. I yearned for the fullers with big fat pricks. My ass brought them a moment's reprieve from the humiliation of slavery. And though I pretended not to like it, in truth, it often felt good to be so completely a slave."

"Were you not humiliated to be used in such a manner?"

"It is a talent. Why should I feel shame? Just as Cook prepares the meals, so I prepare my bottom to be of service." But deep down, I knew Longinus was right. Being used was bad for my humors. The sex was far more pleasure than shame. The scales balanced. Until he came along. From the moment I dressed his wounds, I wanted to be with Longinus. Even before he filled me so completely.

Longinus continued to question me. "You were the very first to take my whole cock down your throat. From what I saw here," he indicated the fullonica, "your mouth is not much in demand. How did you learn to be such a talented cocksucker if these slaves take only your anus?"

He was bound to find out anyway. I heaved a sigh. "The piss bucket is a meeting place for men who want someone to clean their foreskin. I am a slave; if they order me, I must do it."

Longinus chuckled. "Surely it doesn't happen often?" My silence told the story.

"How many dicks do you suck in a day?"

"Ten, more or less."

"And what do they pay you?"

"Slaves are not paid. You know that."

"Oh, Formosus, you sweet, helpless man. Run your fingers across my chest."

It felt massive, like everything else about Longinus.

"Now squeeze my arm."

Two hands were not enough when he flexed. He held out his palm.

"If this is not crossed with silver, I will give the man this." He closed his palm, forming a fist as big as my face. "The gods took pity on us both, boy. You and I will buy our freedom ten dicks at a time."

❧ 6 ❧

THE ALPHABET

His business proposition was fair enough. From now on, he accompanied me to the buckets. If anyone wanted their dick sucked, Longinus would step in and demand payment. And he purposely would wear no loincloth to drum up interest in our private shows. After a long night of anal intercourse, we fell asleep sometime before dawn, wet with each other's juices. The cock crowed far too soon.

Longinus smeared pig fat in my hole. It wasn't just for him. It was for our customers.

Tonight, we would be discreetly borrowed away from Porcius to entertain at the Villa Saturnus. But now he needed my services. I gave them quickly and efficiently. He held me from behind and kissed me while digging ever deeper into my anal cavity. The pressure was tremendous. Clear fluid dribbled from my dick. Longinus caught the essence on his thick hairy finger and sucked it like a peach pit.

We didn't have time for a proper sexual congress, so this was abbreviated. Longinus wiped the sweat from his brow and under his armpits, wiping it on my face. The musky scent drove me wild. My sphincter clamped hard and released a dozen times in rapid succession. I reached over my shoulders until I found both of his nipples. He snorted like a bull. His cock swelled inside me. My anal spasms prevented the erectile blood from exiting his ballooning cock. It felt like a sheep's bladder inflating with hot water deep in my cavernous hole.

When Longinus took my tiny penis between two giant fingers, I could bear no more. Despite its small stature, my little cock was a shooter. It rained cum all over us. Longinus leaned around and lapped up come from my waist. I pinched his nipples hard enough to make him grunt. In response, he increased his pace until it felt as though a hummingbird were flapping its giant cock wings deep inside me.

The growl was a sure sign we were going to arrive on time. It grew louder, like an angry dog protecting his owner's property. Without words, he shoved himself in all the way, pulling me tightly to him by the waist. His breath blew hot on my neck. He stopped moving.

I felt a series of upward thrusts where the base of his cock was stretching my hole. They were a much larger version of the cum muscle twitch that told me my time was up with Porcius or Crassus or any other slave, big or small. In the instant following that twitch, they would flood my anal cavity with their seed. With Longinus, the twitch was a huge spasm. Next, there was a delay, like a flash of lightning followed by thunder. His sperm had such a long journey to make. To ejaculate, he would need a lot more semen, and it traveled a great distance. Luckily, Longinus was blessed with gigantic balls to match his cock. They contracted, sending wave after delicious wave of his come through the penis and deep inside my belly. It was warm and strong. I could feel my body absorbing his essence. He stood, allowing the massive hose of flesh to drain into me. Unlike most men, who have a mere drop or two still trapped inside, Longinus had several full helpings that needed to find their way inside me. This was why we stayed together so long after sex: he needed me to drain him. He had gruel for breakfast, and I ate a full cup of his semen. It made hairs poke from my chest and gave me the strength to carry four buckets of piss.

Our first bucket proved fruitful. A wealthy Jew extended a long, circumcised cock, pissing until the bucket was full. He saw me and snarled, "I need a cleaning." He grabbed my hair, but a much, much larger hand covered his.

Longinus was intimidating. The Jew tried to back away, but Longinus put an arm around his shoulders.

"Fear not. I mean you no harm. What type of cleaning service did you need?"

The Jew stopped trembling. "I wanted him, not you!"

"Formosus? Of course. This isn't for everyone." He grasped his meat through the tunic. The Jew's eyes were drawn to the monster momentarily but returned to me.

Longinus continued his sales pitch. "I didn't catch your name, sir."

"Baruch."

"Baruch, I'm Longinus. Before you stands the most talented mouth and softest ass in Rome. Five gets you both. Three denarii for one or the other."

Baruch cleared his throat. "Two denarii for his mouth."

The Jew's penis was long and plump. It looked weird without the hood, but it tasted much cleaner. He was long enough to pass my tonsils. He gave a surprised yelp when I buried my face in his crotch and stroked his skinless head with the sides of my throat. His wife must never have done that for him. I saw him look to the sky, to his lonely God, and thank him. Tears were in his eyes. The fat, juicy Jewish sausage tasted good. Soon, my mouth grew salty with his pre-come.

He wrapped his thin fingers around my head and held himself all the way in. Then a hot splash signaled his arrival. Unlike most Romans, Baruch did not pull himself free to paint my face. He bypassed my mouth and shot directly into my food pipe. My stomach gurgled with anticipation.

He released me. I took a huge breath, then continued to suck him. This was the "cleaning service" that comes at the end of a good piss and a quick orgasm. I rode his softening pole with my mouth, removing all traces of ejaculate. I released him, and his plump cock smacked into his thigh.

"Two denarii was unfair," he said. Longinus prepared to argue, for a seller must stick to the price once agreed upon. But we misunderstood. He produced five denarii in mixed coinage. I stood and bent forward, lifting my tunic to expose my round bulbous bottom.

"No, dear Formosus," said the Jew, "I only like a cleaning. I don't like digging in the mud. Keep it—job well done.

Longinus held out his hand to me. I surrendered the denarii to my big, strong protector.

He held up a Sestertius and inspected it. "Formosus, What coin is this?"

"It's a sestertius. See, right here on the front."

There was an awkward pause. He cleared his throat. "Thank you"

He couldn't read. I asked him about it on our way to the next piss pail.

"In Thrace, we use only a few of the same letters. I need to learn the Roman alphabet," my protector admitted.

"And I shall teach you. See the arrow?"

I pointed to a sign for the Colosseum. It wasn't even finished, and Rome, in its efficiency, had created signage. I did love a city that cared for the people.

"Let's spell it out. The first letter sounds like your Kappa."

"Kuh."

"Do you see the next letter? It is the same as your Omicron."

"Ko..." Longinus sounded it out.

"Think of this next letter as a lambda tipped over."

"Kolo" He was fast; he recognized O again."

"What do you think the next letter might be?"

The Thracian hulk gave it some thought." It occurs twice."

"What animal does it look like?"

"A snake."

"Yes. So, this is the same as your sigma, which sounds like...."

"A snake! Koloss...colosseum!"

He studied the other letters. It was such a simple pattern. It helped that a few letters were the same, or very similar, in both alphabets.

When we got to the next bucket and had set down our cargo, he lifted me to his mouth and kissed me passionately. "The gods show us favor, for each teaches the other."

I nodded. Held aloft, my front pressed tightly to his; I felt a stirring in my tiny loins.

His long log of flesh plumped and lifted in response. Although Nobiles and Plebeians alike stared at our free preview, none stopped to inquire. I believe they saw something between us that could not be torn apart.

Most men are impressed by size. We stopped at the final bucket. It was empty, so Longinus lifted his tunic and peed. He had no need to aim. He was so heavy; the flow did not cause his massive penis to sway. A crowd formed. Longinus had drained himself, but the onlookers excited him. He swelled until he was half hard. He squeezed the spongy flesh of his bloated tube to force the final drops of urine to the tip. He shook hard, raining big drops of urine into the piss bucket. Men rubbed themselves under their tunics and togas, watching with a mixture of desire and self-loathing. They could never measure up to Longinus Megas of Thrace.

❈ 7 ❈

STOMPING

We returned to the fullonica with eight buckets. We emptied them into the Orinari and sent Gaius away. We would move the clothing through at a gallop. The owner, Porcius, made a surprise appearance at the Orinari, where Longinus and I stomped linen side by side. He frowned.

"Does this job require two slaves?"

I was about to eagerly tell him how much more efficient we were when working together, but Longinus stayed me with his hand.

"The urine collector helps stomp the fine stains from the tunics. I am the muscle to get out the general filth."

Porcius nodded. "I see. Well, you made an impression on the Saturni. They have stains and wish you to bring your services into their home." Longinus and I shared a silent glance.

"Why isn't the urine collector out now?"

"He just returned, sir." Longinus was a smooth talker.

"Then this should be your break...Laomedon, is it?"

"Longinus, master. And I don't take as many breaks because..." He trailed off and flexed a bicep.

"I can see the gods did not overlook you." His eyes

indicated the tunic, erupting with each stomp because Longinus had no undergarments save for a leather pouch he hung from his waist. There he kept our gold, silver, and copper.

Longinus smiled and subtly changed the pace and angle of his stomp to begin a windmill-like rotation. "The gods give blessings but take away liberties."

Porcius was amused. I was amazed at how articulate Longinus was without having yet learned to read the Latin tongue. He must have an incredible mind. Right then, I was hypnotized by the smaller mind at the end of the swinging sausage that Longinus had just employed to keep Porcius in line.

"You are both relieved of duty. The Saturni are paying a handsome sum, quite out of proportion to your value, and I cannot allow such an opportunity to slip from my grasp. Do you know the Villa Saturnus on the Esquiline?"

I nodded.

"Please report to them at once, both of you. Bring a full bucket of urine and a small sackcloth of Fuller's earth. The aqueduct passes directly past their window, so there will be no shortage of water.

Longinus said, "Did they say what we would be cleaning?"

Porcius lowered his voice to a whisper. "There are some bed linens and undergarments that are, well, soiled in a rather embarrassing manner. Apparently, the husband had taken a cold in his stomach, and the contents found their way out rapidly in both directions. This will not be a pleasant job. I found that a little milk will help with stubborn stains." Porcius handed over a tiny milk bottle. "Use it sparingly. I am proud to have such fine slaves as you two. You will make your master rich!"

Longinus grinned as Porcius walked away.

With a shock, we were drenched in cold urine.

Crassus Incommodus laughed cruelly, holding a bucket in triumph. "I know you are scheming against the master. I won't tell him if you let me fuck your boy."

Longinus remained calm. "Crassus, since I know of no scheme, you must first tell me what you know."

"Nice try, Longinus. That is for the master's ears."

"He will hear only an empty wind, you fool. On the other hand, should I let him know that someone doused his two highest-earning slaves in urine without providing them a bath and clean tunics to wear to visit one of the richest households in Rome, I imagine he would be quite upset."

Crassus grunted like the sow he was. And indeed, we were given fresh tunics and coinage for admission to the Thermae, which Longinus added to his leather waist satchel. I felt giddy at the sound of the tiny coins chinking against our substantial loot. In the meantime, Crassus was obliged to bring two buckets of fresh water from the aqueduct to rid us of the foul stench. I marveled at Longinus's bravery and skill at defeating an enemy so foul as Crassus Incommodus.

❈ 8 ❈

THE BATHS

The Villa Saturnus was an enormous estate on the Esquiline hill, close to Nero's Golden House, the mile-long atrocity that wasted more land than any other structure in Rome, Colosseum included. We had to pass through the Forum and ascend a steep incline to get there. We were sweaty and out of breath when we reached the top. Being such a giant, Longinus demanded we take water from the public fountain and rest before continuing. He sat down on the stone fence, spreading his legs to air out his parts. The odor was powerful and intoxicating. I suggested we use the coins to go to the Thermae of Nero.

Longinus was a very practical thinker. "In the baths, I will see your naked body. I will douse you in scented oil and clean your body in all manner. I will not be able to stand it. I would need to take you to a quiet room and fuck you. Then our performance at the Villa will be lackluster."

I countered. "Let us suppose you could withstand the desires of the flesh. Perhaps you could cool your hot irons in the frigidarium. What then?"

Longinus smiled. "My fully erect cock will attract many more future customers."

"Yes, and how will it affect our performance?"

"The delay will double or triple my issue."

I winked.

The Baths of Nero were over 25 years old. They were slated for demolition to make way for a maxi-bath. These giant complexes were popular in the provinces, but none had been built yet within the gates, where land was scarcer than gold.

The Nero complex was small, nearly a mere balneum, but it had all the basics.

Walking naked from room to room, I saw a hundred rheumy eyes gazing at my delicate frame and button penis. More than one old man became erect. For the man who enters a boy, a small penis is quite beautiful. Boys with big endowments rarely inspire lust in masculine old men. Only a gigantic penis like Longinus's excites them, but for a different reason. Seeing me, they feel powerful and aggressive. Seeing Longinus, they become submissive and excited to be close to something so magnificent. Many wish to worship his phallus, for the gods may favor them with more sex and power. Everyone in between is unexciting to them.

Longinus, too, became engorged. In the light of the caldarium, he looked twice as big as I remember. We began to sweat because of the heated floors, so we applied oil to one another. As a crowd formed, I took extra care with his throbbing penis, oiling it generously several times before softly scraping it with the sigil. Longinus focused on my chest and arms. The crowd of perhaps a dozen old men touched themselves and inhaled us into their imaginations, where we could do much more.

Longinus spoke. "We hope you are enjoying the performance." Just those words sent a few timid men running to the frigidarium. He continued. "As you can imagine, this yearns for release. And only he can handle it."

I nodded and pointed to my mouth and buttocks.

"But we will not be doing that here. Can anyone guess why?"

A few smartasses tried a guess.

"You're impotent."

"You have the curse of Venus."

"Your wife won't allow it."

"His wife won't allow it." A finger pointed at me. Lots of laughter erupted at my expense. I was learning from my protector. I steeled my emotions, and the mocking of my passivity fell on a hard shell. I continued scraping dirt from the endless tube of flesh.

Longinus silenced them. "All good guesses. No, the reason is much more exciting. We are performers, and tonight we have an important show in a nearby Villa."

A hush fell over the room. I felt confident, so I broke the silence.

"You won't see me take him in both ends tonight. Someone has already paid for that privilege."

"But," Longinus added, "There is no reason you could not see the show in the comfort of your home. Or at a tavern or bath of your choosing."

Murmurs grew among the crowd.

"How much does it cost?"

Longinus was a true merchant. "What would you pay to see this beautiful bottom and this beautiful mouth invaded by this savage destroyer?"

Someone said, "One denarius?"

Longinus laughed. "24 more denarii and you might get a show you will never unsee. It has caused wives to faint and husbands to seek out pleasure with boys to regain their manhood."

"How much for just the boy?" Asked Ursus, a stout, hairy man with his cock standing straight up against his furry belly. The short fat cock was thick enough at the head, but the base was over two hands thick - a greater circumference than Longinus's. It resembled a Modiolus cup.

"Twenty denarii for just the boy. Sweetest ass and softest mouth in Rome."

"How much for you?" Asked a thin man of perhaps fifty years with pale skin.

I let my ire take over, "He's mine; you can't have him. Besides, what would you do with him?"

Luckily, my temper tantrum had the effect Longinus wanted.

"Yes, I'm afraid he's right, sir. It would be a waste...."

"Two Aurea." The pale man crossed his arms. "For a solo performance. This little cunt can watch, too."

Soon, we were busy whores selling off our bodies, determining meeting places and what to say to Porcius to free up our schedule...it took an hour or more. Our dance card was filled.

✦ 9 ✦

VILLA SATURNUS

The Villa Saturnus was atop the Esquiline, with a perfect view of the massive new Colosseum. The new arena was still under construction, but it would be complete in a year. It was the largest structure in the known world. And we were about to bring to the Villa another splendid view, that of the largest penis in the known world.

The grounds were unlike any public garden. Every plant was arranged in a pattern, creating squares, circles, and triangles built of nature. Running through the courtyard was a narrow rectangular pond with a wide circle in the center. It was Saturn eating his children—water sprayed from the places where Saturn's teeth met the fat leg of a child.

"Kronos," Longinus whispered.

"Saturn."

The Saturni came to greet us.

"Do you like it?" The wife, Drusilla, gestured to the masterful landscape.

We both nodded.

Otto, the husband, handed us each a goblet filled with wine. We toasted. The wine was strong. I felt better immediately.

Otto was very affectionate with me. Drusilla put her

hand on Longinus with more than just a casual touch. They gave us an Aureus for this, so it was their show.

Longinus skillfully moved the conversation into a large living room designed for hosting large parties. There were many soft pillows and chairs to occupy. But Otto and Drusilla sat with us on a single divan.

Otto stroked my minuscule genitalia through the tunic. With his other hand, he reached under and put a finger in my butthole. "That a boy so beautiful be enslaved at a fullonica breaks my heart."

Drusilla echoed his sentiment with Longinus, who, despite her persistence, was not aroused. "One of the most virile men in Rome should not be collecting piss buckets."

There was not much to say in response. "Male captus, bene detentus." Wrongly captured, properly detained.

"Such cynicism from a slave caused Drusilla to erupt in laughter. Otto joined in, and for the next few minutes, we let the wine take us to new levels of joy and laughter.

Once our mirth had died down to infrequent bursts, Otto took command.

"I have examined Formosus, and I find he is to my liking. I shall pay an additional ten denarii for the privilege of warming his trail for you. To my surprise, Otto lifted his toga to reveal a very long penis. It was of an average thickness. It looked like a house snake.

"I cannot have full sexual immersion with Drusilla; her cunt is too small. Sadly, she doesn't like anal intercourse."

Longinus cleared his throat. "We were under the impression that this would be a performance."

Drusilla spoke, "It will be. But upon being in your company, we want to add to the performance."

I remembered that all the oiling and cleaning in the

caldarium had caused me to expel the bulk of the pig fat. I did, in fact, need warming up.

"Longinus, I could actually--" he held a finger to silence me.

"Ten Denarii will only get you the mouth. It's fifteen for the anus. Twenty for both."

"Fifteen is fine." Otto presented Longinus with a stack of coins.

I learned so much from Longinus. The art of negotiation was something new to me. He was naturally skilled in the merchant arts. Perhaps his yearning for gold from his youth never stopped.

Otto looked at Drusilla. "Darling, does Longinus have anything you want?"

"I'm afraid it's too much of what I want."

"I know you like the thick ones."

"I detest excessive length. It is dangerous."

I looked at Longinus and saw his face grow troubled again. But it was a passing cloud. He looked relieved. I can only imagine he never wanted to be with a woman again.

The bedroom upstairs had a balcony open to the stars. Below, the Colosseum sat next to the Forum. Candles burned in many shop windows and houses nearby. It was breathtaking.

Otto whispered, "I am a gentle lover, who will carry you to new places, but you will still need something to make the journey smooth."

I whispered back, "I lost my ointment at the Baths of Nero."

Otto nodded. He presented me with a small stone pot with a locking lid. Inside was a clear ointment that smelled unusual.

"What is it?"

"An oil made from stone. It melts on the skin but remains like butter in the open air." He lovingly applied it to my sphincter and inside my anus, then used much of it to cover himself.

"Stone oil?"

He nodded. "What better than a stone to protect and shield you from harm?"

Until now, he had been doing these many things to me under my tunic. I pulled it off over my head and spread apart the cheeks of my buttocks to give Otto a good view. It worked. His cock lifted off his lap and stretched. It was not any thicker, but it had grown in length.

Longinus sat on the balcony and monitored our activity. He wasn't as jealous as I wanted him to be. I was a mere commodity to him tonight.

Drusilla lay naked beside us. It was disturbing. She said, "He will reach a place past which no penis can go. It's a dead end."

I smiled to myself. I was going to give this couple a real gift tonight.

Otto pressed easily inside me. Girth made sex difficult, and he had no such difficulties. The length was easy to manage for a talented boy like me. I toyed with him. He was being so gentle that it seemed he wasn't even there. I smiled and made sighing noises like a woman. He liked it. When he reached the "dead end," he stopped and began to reverse.

"No, Otto, stay there." I held his exposed cock flesh with my hand and pressed inward. I twisted to one side, and he passed through the rectum into my belly.

"I've punctured you!" he shouted.

"No, it continues. No punctures."

I am confident I saw tears. He had never been here. He slid the last third of his cock into me. I pointed to the side of my belly, where his cock head pressed outwards. "That's you."

Drusilla gasped.

Otto was possessed by the moment. Suddenly, he

wanted to take me roughly. I was glad because his gentle style bored me. Unfortunately, he wasn't thick enough to make me release that clear sticky fluid from my tiny penis. But being snaked deep with Otto's cock brought me great pleasure. Otto rapidly pistoned his cylinder in my anus. If I were a pump, I would be filling buckets quickly. I knew I would make him happy, but the joy I saw on his face was far more than I could have predicted. He slowed, then rested.

"I'm out of breath. I want Longinus here."

Longinus stood, his formidable meat swinging from side to side under his tunic.

Otto asked, "Can you enter him at the same time? I want to rub against your massive cock."

Longinus looked at me for a cue. He saw in my face the easy pleasure Otto had given me. I nodded.

Otto enjoyed emptying the contents of the stone pot, covering Longinus's formidable cock. He couldn't coat the entire surface but got all the essential parts.

Without even coming close to falling out of me, Otto rotated me so that I sat in his lap, facing away from him. He lay back, holding my chest and ankles, and I was pinned on my back. Otto pumped upward in short strokes.

I understood this new position when I felt Longinus press at my hole. He was standing at the edge of the bed. It was a straight shot. When he broke past the first ring, I wanted to scream to stop. It was pain unlike any I had ever experienced. But I knew he would stop if I screamed, and we would lose money.

"Oh fuck." It was all I could say. I said it like I was in ecstasy, even though quite the opposite was true.

Under me, Otto said, "Oh yes, yes, by the gods, yes!" I realized how erotic it was for him to be clamped tightly inside me, benefitting from the great girth of his rival. Longinus was like a bully pressing him against the wall as he plowed further into me. He smiled at me, and

I brought him to me. We kissed deeply. I knew well that he was not close to reaching the end. He slithered around the door that Otto held open for him. In a few more seconds, I felt him pass Otto and reach his deep spot. When I leaned toward Longinus again, Otto did, too. Our lips met in a three-way kiss. I heard a loud moan. It was Drusilla. Our kiss had brought her to climax.

The pain was no longer quite so terrible. Otto's rhythm was different but complementary to that of Longinus. Otto began to flail beneath me. He stopped fucking in an effort to stem the tide, but it was no use. Longinus was fucking the entire length of Otto's dick, and I could feel it grow and pulsate with impending climax. This was the performance they wanted.

Drusilla whispered, "What are the sounds Otto makes?"

I turned to her, "He is getting dick-fucked all up and down my ass." She fell back on the bed and rubbed herself to another climax.

Longinus was only getting started, and his pace was increasing. Otto had stopped his thrusts to prevent climax but couldn't hold back any longer. He fucked me hard for three or four strokes, then stopped again. This time his toes were curled, and his eyes closed tightly. "Oh shit, I'm coming, I'm coming."

And he was. The excitement of being trapped tight inside my hole may have been why he shot so many times. I felt the fluid accumulate like my gut was a teacup. Because Longinus was filling me beyond capacity with his huge cock, I would have to wait to see how much cum I had milked out of Otto.

Otto pulled out with much difficulty. Longinus held Otto captive the whole way out. Longinus was not going to exit me any time soon. He finally pulled his head through my anus with a pop. He licked the tip of his cockhead to catch a few drops of trapped come.

He whispered in Drusilla's ear. She shook her head. He pleaded with her silently. At last, she nodded. And Otto took what I taught him and shoved it up her ass. Her look of surprise when he rounded the corner was worth all the effort. She stared into my eyes. We bonded, both of us getting fucked deep by the men. She reached out a hand, and I took it.

In barely a whisper, she said, "Thank you."

When I turned back to Longinus, he gave me that winning smile. "You got fucked twice at once." I laughed. "It was great. We should do it more often." He grew serious and forced his way in and out of me with great purpose and desire. In this soft bed, probably more expensive than a house in my village, I took advantage of the luxury. I wrapped my legs around his waist and used my feet to press him harder into me. It gave me a feeling of control in a situation where I had none.

Otto spoke. "Can you please take very, very long strokes? We both want to see the head of your penis."

We were paid performers, so we did as requested. The constant exit and re-entry hurt, but it looked incredible, even from my angle. It was as though he walked away to get a glass of water when he stepped back to allow his head to exit me. And then suddenly, he stepped forward to snake his way through my bowels, and I felt his pubic mound on my hole. The pain subsided, as it often did when we fucked. It was now a thrilling awakening of my anal walls, the vagina effect. All the nerves were bringing me to orgasm. I twitched. Longinus knew he was doing the right thing. He kept at it, picking up pace, and I began thrashing from side to side.

A rivulet of clear fluid cascaded down my tiny testicles and onto the bed. I wiped it and fed it to Longinus. I wiped again; Otto and Drusilla licked my hand. The tongues on my hand were extremely sensual. They made the lining of my rectum quiver hard like it had been stung by a wasp. I seized up around Longinus, and his dick benefited greatly. He was in a tightly closed tunnel; each new stroke made the tunnel loosen and then tighten. I looked into his eyes. He nodded. I nodded. Here was the finish, but to get there, I had to relax and let him do all the work. I released my legs from around his waist. He grabbed them and put them on his shoulders. He pinned me down, so I wouldn't go anywhere while he hammered me hard and fast. Oh, the sweet pain of it.

I gaped open, allowing him to enter and exit with full permission. We probably would have fallen off the bed if he weren't holding my shoulders. The constant thick pressure and relentless pounding succeeded in bringing me to orgasm. With my hands holding on to Longinus, I came. It was a spectacular show. I felt like the fountain of Saturn in the courtyard. Left, right, on my face, on Longinus's face, probably on Drusilla and Otto, who were in a new bliss all their own.

Drusilla had three loud orgasms. Otto had his second. It was the first time he had been able to fuck his wife to the hilt.

They turned and watched as Longinus continued to pound me. I surprised myself with a second orgasm. I didn't know it was in there. When a drop landed on Longinus's nipple, I reached up a hand and wiped it. That brought everything to a conclusion.

"Oh, ohh, oh, ohh." His chest heaved as his hips thrust deeply. "Oh, fuck, Formosus, I'm going to come!" He made a sad face and I thought he was crying, but it was a face leading up to full release.

"Here it comes. You want it?"

"Yes, oh yes. Give it to me."

And he did. The come was fiery hot, for much friction had built up in my hole. It felt like the warmest bath at the Thermae. In wave after wave of ball tensing power, my hole filled with the fiery hot soup of semen and cream.

"It's so hot, it scalds," I said.

Longinus grabbed a fluted silver bowl and held it under me as he withdrew his beast from my butt. Drusilla and Otto watched in awe as the bowl filled, giving off steam like actual soup. It was a mixture of Otto and Longinus in the bowl.

I turned to Otto. "Drink it. You will grow even richer."

Drusilla snatched it from me and greedily drank from the bowl. She handed it to her husband, who finished it.

10

THE PRICE OF FREEDOM

Returning to the fullonica, Longinus and I discussed our future.

"We made thirty-five Denarii tonight," he said.

"Forty," I corrected.

"Did you like the job?"

I said, "You mean having sex with you, the best fuck on Earth? What do you think?"

"First of all, Formosus, you are the best ass and mouth, so it's probably not me."

I shrugged.

"What I'm asking is if you want to keep at this."

"Slaves can't spend money. We're not even allowed to earn it. Why are you doing this?"

Longinus grinned. "What is the one thing a slave can buy?"

"I don't know."

"Freedom."

His words brought me to a halt.

"How much would we need, Longinus? I mean, to buy our freedom?"

"I could probably fetch a better price for you as a freedman. I would come back for you."

Longinus wasn't hitting me, but my eyes filled with

tears. It was much worse. He saw the tears and cleared his throat.

"Formosus, did I say something wrong?"

I came back at him with venom, "You use me to get what you want, and then I just have to believe you're coming back for me?"

"What have I done to make you doubt it?"

I wiped the tears from my face. "You hold all the coin."

"We live in a den of thieves. I don't want you to lose your half."

"If that pouch contained 'my half,' then you wouldn't go free first." I folded my arms defiantly.

"Formosus, I would buy you and set you free. It costs half as much as buying your freedom. That means we could make a home together as free men much more quickly."

Longinus made sense, but I was too used to mistrusting everyone around me. I probed deeper.

"Oh yeah, where is this home?"

"During Greek military service, my closest friend was Fortis Teres. He, too, is from Western Thrace, which is now Greater Greece. He told me of a nearby city in Campania. It was founded by Greeks, and they disregard Roman rule. That is where I would build our house."

I was intrigued. He said 'our' house. "What's it called?"

It's called "New City." In Greek, Neapolis.

STRETCHES

Porcius was surprised by the number of requests he got for the two fullers who performed miracles removing stains. He figured the Saturni made a lot of recommendations. When I went to see him, he said that Ursus Faustulus needed us to remove wine stains from his drapes and had paid Porcius a denarius for the service.

Ursus Faustulus was that hairy man at the Nero Baths with the modiolus-shaped cock. I would need to do many stretches to handle such a round, thick tool.

When I mentioned it to Longinus on our bucket haul, he laughed. "You have the best ass stretching tool at your disposal, any place, any time."

He was right. I spied a dark alleyway and put my hand on his firm, round bottom. Our ability to know what the other was thinking had grown in the months we had worked together. This made things better in our business dealings but also in bed. My hand on his butt meant, "Stretch my hole in that alleyway right now."

A moment later, I felt his hands lift my tunic and his thick head press against my hole. I nodded, and he entered me. I writhed with pleasure. The tingling that turned into trembling now started immediately upon penetration. It caused my legs to give, but he already knew that and held me by the waist as he entered me. He knew my sounds of pain and discomfort were just that - sounds. I was so used to him inside me; the pain vanished as quickly as it came. There was no room for such agony when the tingling grew. It was an overabundance of pleasure. It erased pain.

Since this fuck was about stretching, Longinus focused on penetration. He removed his head most of the way and then moved it back in, leaving his long shaft exposed. It was the thickest part of his cock, and the best tool to do stretches. Focusing on the head would make for a shorter experience. He loved to plunge in deeply and spend a long time inside me. Pushing his head back and forth through my rings was too much stimulation for him and always made him come faster. Thinking about my tight sphincter bringing him pleasure was enough to move me past the precipice. I touched my penis, and it exploded.

Longinus felt cum on his leg.

"Did you?"

I nodded.

When I turned to look back at him, he was pinching his nipple. He shook with impending orgasm and thrust himself in. The sudden feeling of fullness forced out even more sperm to paint the wall in front of me.

"Again? Oh shit! Formosus. You beautiful, beautiful boy. Oh, oh!!!" And a Tiberian flood filled my chamber. He held me close from behind, nibbling on my earlobe like Saturn having an appetizer. I felt his hard nipples brush against my shoulders. I kissed the hands that clasped me to him. I can't say how long we stood locked together. We had work to do, so I unclenched and released him. He was still hard. Either we were going to have to fuck again, he was going to have to pull out, or we had more time to wait for him to soften. The soft exit was the most pleasant, so we waited. His hardness diminished, and he became flexible. My bowels did the rest, shitting his cock and a big puddle of cum out my backside. It felt much better than it sounds.

URSUS

That night, we climbed the hill to see Ursus Faustulus. Like his name, he was a big bear of a man. He greeted us at the door with a clay censer of some kind. It smelled strange. A green weed was burning inside one end. He drew a deep breath from the other end, inhaling smoke. He blew the smoke in our faces. Immediately, I felt disoriented. He poured bottomless glasses of wine and insisted we try the weed pipe. With each puff, I felt inhibitions walk away. I glanced at Longinus, who swayed on his feet and gulped wine. Our glasses were refilled several times while Ursus asked us about our work for Porcius.

"Let's not talk of such hardships," said Longinus, "For we are here to celebrate our bodies."

Ursus was drunk and very deep in smoke. He said, "Tonight, I celebrate the body of this young lad. I'm not quite sure why you are here."

I saw Longinus ball his hands into fists. I was drunk and very dizzy, but I rescued the evening. "Longinus is my protector. Besides, you never know; you may want to try a larger cut of meat after the initial banquet." Longinus and Ursus burst into laughter. They led their goblets aloft, waiting for me to join them. Ursus gave the toast, "To good wine, good meat, good weed, and good sex."

I removed my tunic and lay down on a very soft bed. Ursus joined me. I could see his excitement growing underneath his toga. He removed it and kissed me gently. His extremely thick cock was shorter than it was wide...at first. In my clouded head, I thought Longinus was blowing air into his butthole, for the cock inflated in both directions. It gained girth and even more length. Sitting before my face was a monster eel. Two hands could not encircle it. It was indeed thicker than Longinus. Mercifully, it was not even as long as my forearm. I knew why he chose me. After seeing me clean Longinus's hard cock, he knew exactly what I had been able to withstand.

Longinus was very drunk, and the smoke had affected him greatly. He pulled out his cock and tugged at it, looking at me with desire.

But I was not his right now. He had sold me for 20 denarii to this strange but sexy man. Ursus tilted my hips and lapped, licked, and sucked at my ass opening. With all the wine and weed, I let inhibitions fly. I moaned and cried, rubbing his hair and stroking his neck. He kept at it, making my bottom a wet sea of saliva. He spat upon his own cock. This time I was prepared. I took a small clay jar out of my pocket and greased Ursus' conical meat pyramid. He was so thick at the base it took up his entire lap.

He lifted and placed me at the top of the pyramid, facing him. We kissed and stroked one another's skin. The head was smaller than Longinus. I popped it in easily. What wasn't easy was the remaining half cubit of flesh that widened at an alarming rate. It was no problem until the halfway mark. His head was at the turn in my ass, and it was so hard, it wouldn't go. I leaned until I was practically upside down, and at last, it gave.

Ursus gasped. I had taught him a new trick. But the open passageway meant that only my legs prevented him from fully entering me. Because I was at an angle, I lost balance and sat, engulfing all of Ursus at once, tearing the skin near my perineum. He let out a cheer of joy, and I held back a scream of unbearable pain. Luckily, Longinus was deep into a wine-fueled fantasy, probably involving me. He didn't see me cry and bleed.

Ursus shouted praises to the gods of wine and sex. He rolled on top of me to make the beast with two backs. A rough hand cupped my genitals and rubbed them. That, along with the wine and the smoke, took my mind off the pain in my torn backside.

I whispered into Ursus's ear. "I fear I may have released some blood on your sheets."

"I hope so. You wouldn't be real if you hadn't. Does it hurt too much?"

I shook my head.

"Good, then this won't either." With wild abandon, he pounded himself into me. He was not someone who got to do this often, but he knew what he needed to do. It stopped hurting and became a non-stop stretching of my insides. The sensation was very different from Longinus, but it felt intensely pleasurable. As my eyes saw the room for the first time, I noticed the rich tapestries and jewel-encrusted mugs. Ursus was rich. He liked me, too. He started using the paternal with me. "Daddy's little boy likes to take Daddy's huge fat cock up inside him, doesn't he?"

I liked this game. "Yes, Daddy."

"My little boy wants his Daddy to stretch his hole wide."

"Stretch me, Daddy."

"Daddy's going to make sure no one ever hears your farts again."

This caused us both to erupt in hysterical laughter. I looked over at my protector. He was sleeping off the wine.

I kissed Ursus with real passion. I felt safe and free with him. He was not a slave. He wanted me to be his little boy.

My guts were churning with the invasion of the monster cock. It was just as difficult as taking Longinus but for different reasons.

I decided to take things further. "Daddy's boy wants to be with Daddy all the time."

Ursus steered it back to his fantasy, "So his little boy can offer his ass to Daddy any time he wants."

I got very boyish. I clung to Ursus with my arms. "Yes, Daddy, whenever he wants. I'll be your little hole whenever you need it." I planted little boy kisses on his neck and shoulder.

"Does my boy want my come in his ass?"

"Give me your come, Daddy."

To help him along, I let go and grazed his nipple with the back of my hand. He jumped, stretching me to my limits. I put both hands on his nipples. His eyes fluttered, and he growled.

His strokes grew longer, and soon I could feel the evening breeze blow in my gaping wide asshole.

"Daddy, my hole won't close!"

He spat in my open hole and plunged back in. "Daddy needs his boy open and ready to serve him any time."

This was so exciting; it made me come. I splattered Ursus with a double dose of big stones from my small slingshot.

He tasted his beard and pounded me mercilessly. "My little boy gave me some juice, so I must give him some in return."

I pinched both nipples hard.

"Oh shit! Oh, fucking Jove. Oh, Daddy's here. He's here. He——"

Months of saved-up cum emptied into my bowels. Ursus kissed my face, my lips, my chest.

"Did I do it right, Daddy?"

Ursus held me tightly. "Daddy is proud of his boy."

It was not reason that drew me to Ursus. It was an irrational need to be somebody's boy again. Longinus was more of a brother to me. We were both living in servitude, clinging to each other to escape. Ursus was already at the top of the mountain, where all was free and safe. He could really rescue me right now.

I didn't want to ask; I wanted him to offer. So I traced circles around his nipples and quizzed him on his life.

"Is your wife out of town?"

"Oh, ha ha, Formosus. I live here alone."

"That must get lonely. Don't you want someone to share in all this luxury?"

He smiled. "Daddy wants his little boy. Every now and then."

That stung. I was wanted on an intermittent basis. Could his love be as steady as Longinus's?

"If you make me yours, I'll be your boy whenever you want."

I couldn't hear Ursus's reply. Longinus snatched me around the middle and pulled me off. Ursus's softening cock came out of me with a loud pop.

The blankets were soaked in blood and cum.

"What did you do to him, you bastard!" Longinus pounded the bed beside Ursus.

Ursus held up his hands. "I made love to him. I thought that's why I paid you."

"Then why is there blood everywhere? You were too rough!" He slapped my face to revive me. "Come on, Formosus; please don't die."

I laughed, which should have helped, but didn't. Longinus smacked me hard.

I winced. "Longinus, please stop; I'm fine."

He sobbed and held me close, his tears running

down my naked backside. They stung when they reached my torn perineum.

Ursus stood. "This is my fault. Neither of you has smoked the green weed before. It plays with your emotions. I apologize and beg your forgiveness."

Longinus was still irate. "That blood is real."

I jumped in. "Longinus, you were in a reverie when it happened. I ripped my skin in a clumsy maneuver."

"I saw blood pour from your hole. Even now, it is a red rosebud."

I looked at my backside in the mirror; he was right.

Ursus said, "As you must have seen, I am bigger around than you." He pressed on the protruding flesh, and it popped back inside me. "The first time, even for someone with Formosus's talent and experience, will always be a bloody affair, I'm afraid."

Longinus nodded. Then he said something entirely unexpected. "I have always wondered how much pain I cause my beloved Formosus. Can you show me?"

Longinus set me down. Ursus gazed into his eyes. "Yes, Yes. I will show you."

Longinus seized his face and kissed it deeply. My Daddy found a new boy. Now it was my turn to watch. I handed my pot of pork fat to Longinus. He applied it liberally.

I felt as though I were watching a chariot race in which one of the wheels would soon come off. Longinus never spoke of ever being on the receiving end of this transaction. Otto or Baruch was the right man for a first-timer. Ursus was not.

Ursus knew this about himself. I was grateful when he asked, "Am I the first to pay a visit to your nether regions?"

Longinus shook his head.

Ursus was good. "Tell me of the others. Who was the longest, and who was the thickest?"

Longinus said, "He was both. Longer than you, but not as thick."

I desperately wanted to interrupt and demand details, but it was not my turn to speak now.

Ursus continued, "Did he force his way in, or did he let you sit upon him and guide the beast into its cave?"

Longinus fought back tears. Whoever he was, he must have been important...though not significant enough to merit a mention to me.

"Please, do what I do to Formosus."

"Forced entry?"

Longinus nodded. Ursus shook his head at me and smiled. I smiled back.

Ursus grew longer and thicker while staring at Longinus sprawled across his bed. He kneeled and placed his knob at the entryway. He leaned forward but didn't enter. He leaned harder, and I could almost hear the sound of flesh passing flesh. Longinus bit down on a cushion and closed his eyes tight. He gripped the sheets and nearly shredded them. He was learning that Ursus had a conical shape; it only worsened. With Longinus, at least the head was the worst part.

Ursus held Longinus by his firm muscular buttocks and pressed further. Longinus cried out, "No!"

Ursus withdrew. Longinus sat on the edge of the bed, his cock resting on the floor. A tiny blossom of red radiated from where his anus touched the sheets. He held his head in his hands.

I put a hand on his shoulder. "What's wrong."

He looked me in the eyes. "How can you allow me to torture you like that?"

"But Longinus, it's not torture."

"Why lie about it?"

Ursus, the wise Daddy, interrupted. "Let me help you both. Listen. Longinus, the gods have crafted each of us to serve a purpose. Consider me. I was blessed with a huge cock that is too big for women. I use it for boys. You, too, were gifted. Your gift far surpasses mine in elegance and symmetry. The gods gave Formosus a beautiful face and a perfect bottom."

Longinus shrugged. "What are you saying?"

To ensure that you used your gift, they gave you intense pleasure when fucking. To further keep you on the right road, they made it painful for you to do the reverse. The gods did the same with me."

"It hurts everyone. It's wrong." Longinus whined.

Ursus asked me, "Formosus, do you derive any pleasure from penetrating a man or woman?"

I laughed and pointed. "Obviously not. How can I?"

"And how does it feel when Longinus penetrates you and brings you to mutual orgasm?"

"I can think of nothing better."

Longinus looked at me in awe.

Ursus concluded, "So you see, there is a place for everyone, and everyone has their place."

Longinus understood. I climbed in his lap and planted tiny kisses on his neck and cheek, then his lips. We kissed deeply, and I felt his log of flesh touch my bottom.

Longinus looked at Ursus. "You earned a free show."

13

REST

I thought I knew a lot about Longinus, but I was uncertain about nearly everything that night. Much of his story was still untold. At the same time, I doubted my own feelings for him. Was he going to leave me stranded? We could never earn enough gold to be as wealthy as Ursus. I was ashamed of how I had fantasized about leaving Longinus for Ursus, the stable Daddy with a fatter cock, greater wealth, and more power. It was a heartless shortcut. Longinus and I could make each other great, and we would not be alone like Ursus. He was a wealthy Plebeian who may have inherited his status and gold from his parents. Longinus, like me, was a slave who had found a way to break free of the bondage so long as we had each other.

What worried me most was the fear and irrational attitude toward blood. Who had he been talking about when he described his own anal experience? I was grateful Ursus explained our place in the universe and how one is meant to submit to the other. I could certainly never give Longinus but a tiny fraction of what he would need should he decide to change positions. While I was deeply lost in my muddled mind, Longinus cleared his throat.

"Formosus, I am sorry for my behavior. I owe you an explanation."

"It's late. I'm tired and confused. Your explanation will be better heard and understood after a night's rest."

Longinus nodded. "Agreed. Perhaps tomorrow on our rounds."

I took hold of his index finger with my small hand to let him know everything was okay. He looked down and smiled. "In nocte consilium."

14

MILITARY SERVICE

The following day, we carried our buckets in lazy circles as we talked. I knew better than to reveal my wish for an "instant Daddy." Longinus must never know how I felt. I didn't betray him in deed, just in my mind. It was my private burden.

Longinus needed to get something significant off his chest. I listened with growing horror as his story unfolded.

"I had no rank in the Greek army since I was a conscript. This meant officers had absolute power over me, like a master over a slave. My, um, endowment was far too large to keep hidden. Most men were amused or fascinated. But one or two felt threatened, including my commanding officer, Aimoboros."

The name made me shiver.

"He was not small down there; in fact, he was quite large. He was among the biggest, but my incredible size knocked him from his pedestal, which was the reason for his cruelty toward me. He was much older than I was at the time, perhaps forty years of age. He invented a job for me: night butler. It was an excuse to torture me. To avoid worse punishment, I agreed to his nightly summons. Taking me off guard, he would force his brutal cock inside me without any oils, not even saliva.

He told me this would ensure I would not enjoy it. He was right. I could not enjoy such intense pain, and my body responded. He would laugh and point at my shriveled penis and say, 'See, you are no great prize. I am far superior, which is why you let me penetrate you.'"

This story opened a window, letting some light enter the dark room that was Longinus before slavery. We were at the first bucket and distributed it equally among our eight. This was a system that allowed us to go much more quickly since we were each carrying small amounts until the end. He continued,

"The pain, blood, and burning were made all the worse for what I felt in my heart."

"Hatred?"

He shook his head. "Love."

I stopped in the street. "How could you feel such warmth for your tormentor?"

"If I could explain the human heart, we wouldn't be slaves. It made no sense. He showed nothing but disdain for me."

I shrugged. "The heart has its own reason and rules."

Longinus smiled. "Aimoboros was horribly cruel without favor. When he showed a moment of kindness, it made you feel like you were an emperor. I lived for those moments of small mercies during those long, painful nights. They grew more frequent until one night, he did the unimaginable - he kissed me."

I told myself that this had happened ten years or more in the past, but the heart's reason prevailed. I was jealous.

Longinus continued his strange tale. "Over the next few months, he offered another drop of kindness every night. Perhaps some olive oil to make the penetration and fucking more pleasant. Another night, it might be not one but two kisses upon my bare shoulder. I gobbled the crumbs of kindness, hoping they would somehow grow into a whole slice of bread. But I under-estimated Aimoboros. He was cold, calculating, and extremely patient.

"What did he do?"

"He told me he loved me."

I laughed. "I tell you that every day. Am I cruel?"

"I hope not. After that, I don't know why, but I wanted to give myself to him. It never felt right. I was always in pain and unable to experience the joy I see on your face, Formosus." He looked sad. "Ursus was right. We are all built for our place in life. But I believed I could learn to like it. I was wrong."

Puzzled, I said. "I never realized it was unpleasant for some men. There is pain, yes, but it is quickly over-taken by ecstasy. Do you never feel this?"

Longinus said, "I may have come close on nights when there were many kisses and lots of olive oil, but most of the time, I couldn't stand it. I only endured be-cause my heart was hopelessly entangled in Aimoboros's web.

"One night, when we were all at dinner, he stood up. 'I have an announcement.' The army fell silent, fearing his wrath. 'There is one among you who has earned a place at the head of the table with me. He could only do this by submitting completely and allowing me nightly egress into his darkest regions. He showed no shame or humility, only complete subservience. He is not a man; he is a worm. I give you the Thracian sex slave, Longinus Megas. Use him for your pleasure.'"

The soldiers laughed and jeered and called me names in Greek that I hope never to hear again. That whole time his love torture had been a game to see my dignity destroyed. Hands came from nowhere, holding my arms and legs. I was still young and had not devel-oped strong muscles. The next in command stepped up. He was well-endowed and brutal. I cried in pain and helplessness.

"I endured a whole night and day being used for everyone's pleasure. Some men tried to take me in their mouth or the anus, but they quickly gave up. I was tied to a bench, my legs spread, and my arms immobilized. There were over a hundred soldiers, and they all needed release. Thankfully, most were small and easy. Some were affectionate, kissing me and stroking my cock until they were done. As my ass filled and overflowed with semen, it grew slick. I could take the very biggest of cocks without pain. But I could find no pleasure, try as I might, for I wanted to be the one doing the fucking."

I put my hand near Longinus's crack and rubbed softly. He smiled down at me.

"I slept twenty-four hours. Then the gods turned the table again.

"What happened?"

"Several things happened. First, he summoned me to his tent like nothing had transpired. He probably believed he could continue the cruel seduction designed to break my spirit. I was not the right person to torture in that way. You have seen me, Formosus; I have a stormy temper. And he had unleashed thunder and lightning."

"Did you go when he summoned you?"

"Yes. I marched past the guards who had grown accustomed to my nightly visits and closed the blankets on the tent. Aimoboros was undressing, his back to me. 'Go lie down, boy; I will come pleasure you in a minute.' His words sent flames of rage across my face. With the strength and fury of a hundred soldiers whose cum I had taken, I grabbed him by the neck and threw him on the bed. I tore his robes and found the hole I needed. Without mercy or lubricants, I plunged in and fucked him so hard and so deep he lost his breath. He couldn't scream, and I choked him to make sure of it. Soon, there was a pool of blood on the blanket. I had been incautious with him, as he had been with me. Unfortunately, my weapon was much bigger and caused more damage. Between tears, I cursed him and told him he was a tick on the asshole of my mother's horse. He didn't respond; he couldn't. I let his throat go, and he caught his breath but held his belly and moaned like a small child. I continued to plunge ever deeper, scraping and tearing my way to the furthest reaches of his bowels. His struggles became weaker, and finally, he was still. When I came inside him, I yelled at the gods. The guards didn't come; that was just the usual sound I made while suffering under Aimoboros. I pulled myself from him in a sudden yank, and with my cock came a deluge of blood, feces, and cum.

I gasped. "Was he—?"

"Dead? Yes. Then, as proof the gods are paying attention, there rose the sound of swords clashing. Burning arrows lit up the tent. The Roman army was much closer than any of us had imagined. Our fortress was in flames. I ran from them and didn't stop until dawn. As I lay sleeping on the river's shore, Charis, a soldier who had been kind while raping me, pulled me into the shade."

"Why?"

"The Roman guard was less than a hundred feet away. We held our breath as they marched past us on the river bank and then vanished around the bend."

Longinus took a deep breath. He and I were at the second bucket, and we had work that required just enough concentration that we could not tell stories.

On the way to bucket number three, Longinus continued. "I asked my new friend what befell the fort. He said that Aimoboros had been run through with a broadsword. I wanted to laugh but couldn't. Not just because I might expose my guilt but also because my heart was broken. Despite all the wretched things Aimoboros had done, I still wanted to love him. As the guilt of having torn him in two with my cock grew more intense, tears fell. Charis held me and asked if I had loved the officer. I nodded. We held each other, not knowing what move we should make to ensure our safety."

"Were you captured?"

"Not until several years later. Charis and I found our way to the sea and became fishermen for a small fleet in Salonica. He proved to be a good friend."

"Did you fuck?" I was ashamed of my jealous mouth.

"We weren't compatible. He preferred to be the woman but could not handle my size. I never wanted another cock in my ass again. We used our hands and our mouths to help one another. It was a friendship between men, not love."

I suppressed my jealousy. The story explained a lot, but not quite everything. I cut to the meat. "Longinus, did you hurt anyone else?"

"I never again met a man or woman who would let me inside them. Not until I met you." He touched my cheek affectionately.

"Really?"

"By Jupiter, I am telling the truth."

"But did you force yourself upon the unwilling?"

Longinus grew quiet. In a whisper, he admitted it was so.

"Who was the lucky lady?"

"He was the son of a fisherman. He wanted to be with me, not me with him."

"Oh, tell me more."

"Nicos was a beautiful lad. I often caught him staring at my tunic where my manhood bowed outwards. He often caught me gazing into his eyes."

I did my best to let the jealousy pass over me like a cloud on a sunny day.

"Nicos had taught himself the talents of the tongue.

He was able to take me partway in his mouth. So any-time we were assigned to a two-man boat, we pleasured one another. He was not small, nor was he large. I easily took him in my mouth. Nicos struggled with me. But long after I had swallowed his semen, he persevered un-til, at last, I returned the favor.

"When the two of us were assigned together with great frequency, I recalled that his father owned the boats. Nicos influenced the assignment of duty."

I looked at my dirty feet and urine-soaked sandals and yearned to be the son of a fisherman. "It sounds good."

"It was perfect...until it wasn't."

"Go on"

"On our last trip together, Nicos brought several jugs of fortified wine aboard. We caught much fish in our nets and were able to quit early and stay out on the sea for many hours of mutual sucking, Nicos may have known, but I had no idea the wine was so strong. After one bottle, we were both inebriated. And we opened a second. We were too giddy with wine and kisses to see the dark storm clouds.

"He struggled to suck me; in my drunken lust, I wrestled him to the deck. He was laughing so loud I didn't hear when the giggles became shrieks of terror. I tore his loincloth and forced myself inside. As I pressed deeper, I heard sobs. I withdrew and saw blood. I held him, crying, apologizing repeatedly. He struggled to get away from me. It was then that the storm was upon us."

I was afraid to hear more.

"I begged Nicos to forgive me, but he threw wine in my face. We were too drunk to sail to shore, so we reefed the sails and rode out the storm. In the middle of the night, the boat flipped. I pulled myself onto the hull. Nicos was gone. I cried myself to sleep, hoping another wave would wash me away. I was cursed. Everyone I loved died when my dick tore them apart. I awoke on the shore ten miles from Salonica. I didn't dare return, so I made my way towards Athens. On the road, I was captured by Legionaries."

I shook my head. "Is that how you wound up on the auction block in Rome?"

Longinus smiled. "Yes, after several years of conscripted service, they brought me to Rome. Slavery was my pension plan. As a Thracian, my military service meant nothing."

At the corner, where we changed our next bucket, I put my arms around his waist and laid my head on his broad chest. "Longinus, you have suffered enough. You have me now. And I have you!"

"I'm so afraid of hurting you, of losing you."

"You can thank our master that my hole is well stretched and happy to accommodate all of you. And it doesn't hurt. It feels so good; you'll never lose me...you'll never be rid of me!"

I felt Longinus grow hard under his tunic. Luckily, we knew of a dead end nearby. After a fierce fucking, my stretched and satisfied hole left a glistening trail of his semen on the cobblestones along our walk back to the fullonica.

❈ 15 ❈
A LETTER

One morning, Crassus woke us up and put us on prep duty. There were dozens of Togas piled up, and they needed to be unfurled to get as clean as possible. As Longinus unfolded the first toga, a scroll fell to the floor. I stooped to retrieve it and handed it to him. He sounded out the letters.

"What does it say?"

"I can't make it out. I'm still learning."

I took the scroll and read with amazement. It was documentation granting free passage with Legionary protection to the bearer. The owner of the toga, Magnus Maximus, would be quite pleased to receive it back. I was about to hand it over to Crassus when Longinus grabbed my arm and pulled me close. He whispered, "This is our freedom."

I countered, "It only grants passage to one Roman Citizen. You are neither."

"Do I not look Roman to you in this toga?" He put on the stained but passable garment and instantly became a Plebeian.

"Where will you go without me? You wouldn't leave me, right?"

"Every Roman needs his house slave to travel with him."

I wanted to be offended, but given my small stature and his commanding presence, it made good sense.

"When do we leave?"

"We need a few months to build up substantial savings."

I reviewed the travel papers. Magnus Maximus had applied for these over a year ago. They were granted three months ago and expire in three months.

"Longinus, we have but three months."

"That's a lot of time if we turn things up. What was the name of that pasty-skinned man at the Nero Baths? The one would pay two Aureis for me to fuck him?"

"I think he was Abyssus Obediaens."

"We're going to pay Abyssus a visit tonight. He offered a tidy sum; Let's see if he makes good."

On our rounds, we stashed the buckets and ascended the Esquiline hill to the house of Abyssus. To our astonishment, he answered his own door.

He ignored me and put both hands on Longinus's arms. "I wondered when you would accept my offer."

To my disgust, Longinus poured on the charm. "I always save the best parts of my meal for the end. Consider it a great compliment."

"Come in; we can get started now."

Longinus smiled. "Can we give you some time to get ready?"

"Oh, you're bringing your little cunt along? I suppose he can watch us and learn. I am world class, Longinus, world class."

'A world-class jackass,' I thought, but said nothing.

"I am a collector of men with your...ample dowry. Whatever your little friend thinks he knows will pale to what I will show you under the canopy."

I forced a smile. It may have looked like a grimace. It didn't matter - Abyssus had no interest in me.

Longinus got back to business. "I am interested in

your skills, but let's talk lucre for a moment. You offered two Aureis. Do you have that much?"

Abyssus laughed. "You haven't heard of me, which is
good, because I don't want people to know who I am
and just how much I have. Two Aurei are nothing
to me."

He bent over, exposing his sallow, flabby buttocks.
He removed a chest from under his bed. Inside were
hundreds of Aureorum.

"This is just my spending money for the month. I
keep the rest locked away with the moneylenders. Fear
not, you will get paid."

Longinus needed to be delicate. "This is your
spending money for one month? What a powerful and
wealthy patron you must be." Abyssus nodded in
agreement.

"How do you come by such wealth?"

Abyssus scowled, then released a smile like a fart. "I
suppose I could tell people of no consequence such as
yourselves. Don't pass this on, not that anyone will believe you. I sell secrets."

"You what?"

"Yes, if the Greek general wishes to know where the
Emperor eats breakfast, I sell him that information.
And if the Emperor wants to know how tight the
Greek general's ass is, I sell him that information too."

"I never realized the tightness of a military man's
bottom was consequential enough to merit payment."

Abyssus laughed. "I do whatever makes men in
power happy."

Longinus said, "Perhaps we should see if there is
something on the menu that will make you even
happier."

"I should like to throw him out of a high window."
He pointed to me. "How much for that?"

If I had a knife, I would have thrown it at him.
Longinus stayed focused on business.

"My life would be very miserable indeed, Abyssus. There is no price you can put on friendship; I'm sorry."

"I wasn't serious. He looked Longinus up and down, then reached under his tunic to unleash the mammoth organ. Touching it made him squeal like a pig."

"It's so much bigger in my hands!"

Longinus nodded.

"I expect two Aurei will cover everything I wish to do with you."

Longinus made his play. "As you can imagine, it requires a great deal of energy to bring pleasure to such a large cock. I wouldn't want to burden you with the many hours required. I will need to return to my workplace before midnight. I don't think it will be enough time—"

"What are you saying? You won't be giving me your seed?"

Longinus smiled. "It can be arranged."

Abyssus looked even uglier than usual. "How much for the gift of your essence?"

"Another two Aurei will suffice."

"Let's make it five, and you will plant your seed in me twice."

Longinus shrugged. "That may take a very long time unless you are a gifted lover."

"Have I not told you I am world class?"

"You did." Out of view, I rolled my eyes at this pathetic old creep.

"You shall see. I will have it out of you twice before the candle burns out, or you will get double. Ten Aureis. All yours if you can remain temperate and hold your second load of seed inside until after the light is spent."

"And if I hold both?"

"I feel quite safe in saying you will never succeed, so I will give you twenty Aurei if you are immune to my charms."

"So, five Aurei for the delivery, so to speak, ten if

one delivery comes after the candle's last light, and twenty if both deliveries come late."

Abyssus nodded. He smiled for the first time, revealing decaying teeth. "I love a good challenge. Your boy, he will watch and learn. Agreed?"

They shook hands, and we returned in silence to our buckets at the bottom of the hill.

Longinus spoke first. "Formosus, you know you are my heart's desire. I think this Abyssus is going to fail. We will have enough gold to buy a house in Neapolis. In one night!"

"I don't get it. How does that worm make his money?"

"He spies for the highest bidder."

"Isn't that dangerous?"

"He's world class; what has he to fear?"

With that, we both burst into laughter. I felt better now that Longinus was free of that worm. His laughter was a tonic for my spirit.

※ 16 ※

PIUS

We worked each corner hard. In the first bucket, we encountered a temple priest. I was astonished by the powerful log of flesh between his legs. The priest saw me staring, and when he had shaken the last drops from his massive tool, he approached.

"Your eyes betray a yearning, boy."

"Yes, sir. I only desire to clean you, for these are my buckets."

"Who is the mastodon who accompanies you? His trunk swings freely."

"He is my protector."

Longinus stepped forward, taking the priest by the arm and steering him into the alleyway. Longinus negotiated my fee. The priest jingled with coin. He collected offerings, no doubt, and spent them on 'necessary' items for the temple.

The priest began to lecture me. "I must warn you; it's very long and not many-- ohh!"

I surprised him with my deep dive. In one quick motion, he was engulfed in my throat. Practicing with Longinus made everyone else seem like child's play.

Longinus stood guard in a wide stance at the entrance to the alleyway. The morning sun shone through his tunic, casting his powerful thighs and cock in silhouette.

I struggled not to look away from the priest and his heavy cock. I buried my nose in his crotch, using my throat muscles to massage him. I hummed a tune to add to the stimulation.

"By his sword, you are talented!" The priest ran his fingers through my hair.

I pulled back for a breath. I said, "I know."

"Any time you wish to practice this and your many other talents with a man of my gifts, you will find me in the Temple of Mars. Ask for Pius. I will reward you handsomely."

I nodded, taking his pendulous Roman meat to the very depths of my esophagus.

In a moment of distraction, I put my hands on his backside. I was surprised at how full and round his buttocks were. He responded to my touch with a series of thrusts that foretold a climax.

"Oh, you beautiful boy. Suck me. Yes. Yes!"

The priest quivered, and his legs buckled. I used all my strength to hold Pius aloft by his plump butt. He was past my tonsils, and the semen shot directly down my throat to my empty stomach. I pulled back and inhaled, milking more and more of the delicious manly essence from his overripe plum of a cock head.

It was another Denarius for our future and the promise of many more if I could find Pius at the Temple of Mars.

I liked the Aurei much more, for it took twenty-five Denarii to equal one Aureus. Tonight's appointment with the unpleasant Abyssus could be worth five hundred acts of fellatio. Longinus was very valuable, with or without me.

At dusk, Porcius told us of an engagement with a 'very foul man' tonight on the Esquiline, close to the Villa Saturni.

"I think Otto Saturno's word travels with some weight. All his neighbors clamor for your stain removal."

I shared a private smile with Longinus.

"High quality is its own best advertisement." Longinus always knew what to say.

❧ 17 ❧

INTO THE ABYSS

We arrived at the home of Abyssus in darkness. He came to the door with a long tapered candle. His smile for Longinus was as cruel as his frown in my direction.

"I didn't dare light it until you arrived. Come." He took Longinus by the arm and led him into a dim bedroom. The door nearly slammed shut in my face had I not caught it with my foot. I rarely felt a deep loathing for a person, but in the case of Abyssus, I made an exception.

Abyssus prattled on, which was fine for us. Every sentence saw the candle grow shorter by a hair.

Abyssus made a sudden advance and began tugging Longinus's cock under the tunic.

"We shall make it nice and hard, hmm?" He was repulsive, but Longinus kissed him anyway. Soon his massive meat swung forward and stood at attention.

I was sent to the dressing room to retrieve an unguent to aid in the insertion. It was a dirty glass jar filled with white fat that was too richly scented to be from a pig.

"It is the oil from the fruit of a palm tree. Your mighty tree trunk will require much."

He crassly scooped out a helping for himself, spreading it in and around his sagging butt.

The sight made Longinus go limp. I took small helpings and rubbed them onto his struggling manhood. The touch of my hands all over his organ gave him renewed vigor. He whispered in my ear, "Remember the candle."

I released my hold.

Abyssus Obediaens snatched the greased meat and placed the head at his asshole. Longinus pressed forward and found himself easily inside. It was an astonishing sight.

"I was once a pretty slave like your friend. There was always something or someone in my ass until I bought my freedom. Now I have to pay for the privilege!"

Longinus pressed on, sliding quickly to where his hips touched the bare buttocks.

Abyssus gyrated and bucked, ensuring every inch was inside him.

"Now fuck me hard. Don't hold back. I need to know you are there."

Longinus obeyed, pounding in short, furious strokes. He feigned a yawn for my benefit.

Abyssus moaned softly. "Oh, that's it. Oh yes."

His tiny shriveled penis grew very big and hard.

"Boy, make yourself useful. Suck my cock."

I looked at Longinus, who nodded.

How disgusting. I placed the throbbing cock in my mouth. I was furious that it was big, beautiful, and tasted good.

Abyssus chided Longinus. "Why do you cling to this little slave with no dick? He can take you, but I can do so much more. I could offer you luxury like you've never had. Give up this worthless cunt, and I will be a good master, showering you with gifts."

Longinus was furious. He rammed harder and

harder. His thrusts caused Abyssus's cock to scrape my teeth.

"Ow! You little bitch! You bit me." He punched my face hard.

Longinus shook his head, silently telling me to stand back. He punched Abyssus in the bladder with his cock. The spy let out a shriek. It turned out to be a cry of pleasure. He wet the bed.

Longinus kept fucking him harder and harder, causing Abyssus to leak more urine and pre-cum on the sheets.

"Oh yes! Oh! Longinus, you animal! Harder!"

I hated Abyssus. The only advantage I had over him was youth and beauty. He had me beat in every other way: money, freedom, a home, a big dick, and a loose hole.

I watched astounded as Longinus lifted one leg and entered Abyssus from the side. Their balls touched. I saw the red rim of Abyssus's anus and, despite my distaste, marveled at its great circumference.

Longinus struggled to find any way to make Abyssus give up and beg for a pause. That had been his strategy, but it wasn't working. He put Abyssus upside down on the ground and fucked downwards. After an eternity, Abyssus finally complained. He was uncomfortable and wanted to do it face to face, "so I can kiss you."

I turned away.

When I looked back, the kiss was over. Abyssus pinched both nipples on the Thracian sex God. He grabbed by the wrists and held his hands away. He humped so hard, I could hear him striking innards and tearing tissue.

Abyssus groaned with pain.

"Are you okay? Shall I stop?"

The sallow old man shook his head. He was in a daze. "No. More."

Longinus sighed and continued his long, battering

strokes. I could see his cockhead move violently across Abyssus's abdomen.

Longinus pulled back hard, and with his dick came a giant pink slug. Abyssus was turned inside out. There was blood. The pink slug undulated and throbbed, burping blood onto the bed.

Abyssus said, "Oh, did I prolapse? That's quite a cock you have, Longinus. Just push it back in and keep going."

I gagged. The sight was disturbing. Longinus put his cock in the mouth of the slug and pushed it back inside. He was defeated. There was no way to make this bottomless pit beg for mercy. The candle was still at half.

Longinus continued to pummel the man's insides. The old spy was groaning more but would not let Longinus stop. He was clearly in pain, but it was what he wanted.

I watched my man closely. He would pound away for a dozen or more strokes, then withdraw his head enough to expose the pink slug. He gagged and pushed it back in. He repeated this cycle over and over. He was purposely making himself sick to prevent accidental orgasm.

Abyssus looked at me. "Lazy little slave. Come over here and stroke my big cock. I'll bet you wish you had one like mine...big enough to fuck."

I stroked his penis with a bored look on my face.

"See, that's a real man's penis. Yours is too small to have a name."

I tightened my grip until he cried out. "Oh, do that again."

I was so repulsed by this man with his money and foul mouth. I looked at Longinus, and he mouthed the words, "I love you." It made me warm inside. I lost focus.

I snapped out of my daydream when Abyssus punched my jaw so hard I saw stars.

"You are on my payroll; you will do as you're told, you little fucking, whore."

Apparently, Longinus had been holding back. The violence he unleashed was tenfold. Abyssus cried for real. "You're hurting me."

"That's what you want, right?"

But the old fart was in too much agony to answer. Longinus didn't care anymore. This man would show respect.

The candle still burned. Longinus decided to throw away ten Aurei for the privilege of hurting this man and leaving early.

"I may come before the candle is out."

I nodded. Abyssus cried and held his abdomen.

Longinus continued fucking violently, and his breath grew fast. His butt cheeks quivered as he pounded the wretched man's hole.

"Oh shit. I'm gonna come."

Music to my ears, even if it meant losing half a house.

But in his violent strokes, he pulled too far, and the entire slug came sliding out. It was bruised and bloody.

Abyssus muttered, "Put it away. It goes inside,"

Longinus gagged as he struggled to replace the horrifying monster that had slid out of Abyssus.

He had to start over. He fucked hard and painfully. Abyssus said very little. Most of it encouraged Longinus to keep at it, so he did.

Soon, it started again. "Oh yeah. Oh yeah. This is it. I'm gonna, oh fuck I'm gonna..."

The candle went out. We were plunged into darkness.

"Ohhhh hohoho Yeah!"

In the dark, I only heard the wet sucking noises as Longinus slid in and out of the unstable rectum.

I looked for a candle with my hands. I found one down the hall and lit it using the fireplace.

When I returned to the room, it looked like a battlefield. Blood and bodily fluids stained the bed.

Longinus thumped Abyssus. "Ready for round two?"

There was no response.

I pointed to his asshole, where his entire rectum was outside, inverted, puking blood and cum in angry spurts.

Longinus used his hand to push it back inside, but it wouldn't stay.

"Abyssus? How do we fix this?"

The old man was unresponsive. His prolapsed rectum leaked black blood. He was not going to survive this. He hiccupped and ejected black blood and bile from his mouth. His eyes turned to glass.

"Longinus, what do we do?"

"Grab that chest under the bed."

18

WAGES OF SIN

Although I had wished many horrible things to befall Abyssus, being fucked to death was not one of them. He was a gutted fish on the banks of the Tiber. Death was already familiar, but causing death was new to me. The look on Longinus's face told a grim story.

"Can I help?"

He was cleaning up the worst of the mess, and I felt useless.

"You have sharp eyes. Tell me if there is blood on my tunic, and help me find evidence that we were here."

"There is some blood there," I pointed to a spot below his waist, "I think it came from inside your tunic. Your cock is covered in it."

He removed the tunic. His dick was indeed covered in thick congealed blood mixed with feces. I got a cloth from the kitchen and soaked it in white vinegar. Tenderly, I held his massive penis in my hands and scrubbed. It took a long time, of course, for there was so much skin needing cleaning, but in the end, his cock, balls, and pubic hair were spotless. I applied vinegar to the bloodstained tunic, but it was stubborn.

I pissed into a bowl and soaked the stains, hoping it

would help. Then I found the tiny bottle of milk that Porcius gave us. I lifted the stained fabric from the urine and soaked it in milk. Instantly, the blood dissolved. With a few more applications, the tunic was good as new. We would need to rinse it in water, but it was clean.

I discovered a pool of fresh water behind the house. Rinsed and wrung, the tunic would not dry quickly in the night air. But the heat of Longinus and his bulging muscles would hurry it along.

We dumped a large quantity of gold into the satchel Longinus wore under his clothes and left perhaps twenty or thirty coins behind so that our robbery would not be as apparent. I put the chest back under the bed. Abyssus lay in his blood and filth, his gaping anus stretched by the prolapsed rectum. I gagged every time I saw it.

The whole process took several hours. We crept back to the fullonica in the moonlight and tried to sleep.

"Longinus, I'm worried."

"You must never speak of this. Ever." He rolled on his side and gave me his back. I rubbed it until he snapped at me to let him sleep. "Your dick really is deadly." I regretted teasing him even before the whispered words left my mouth. For the first time, Longinus smacked me hard. I don't recall drifting off to sleep, but I remember waking to a great deal of commotion.

The vigiles were questioning Porcius. Someone had left milk and fuller's earth at the house of a murdered spy, and the fullonicae were the first places they did their questioning. I cursed myself, for it must have been me who left it there. I shook Longinus awake.

Porcius answered the vigiles as best he could. Yes, he had two slaves who visited the house that night, but they returned early.

Then Crassus hissed like a snake, "They didn't return until the wee hours of the morning. And their purse was full."

Longinus stashed the bag of gold in the first place he could find - a dirty chamber pot. The vigiles barged in on us with Crassus in tow.

"Look under his tunic; you will see he has it tied to his leg," spat the evil slave.

A vigile with flaming red hair accosted us. "Where were you last night?"

Longinus answered, "We were at the house of Abyssus Obediaens for about the length of a candle. We departed with our cleaning supplies when the moon was high."

Crassus interrupted. "Lies! Lies and deceit! You are a murdering thief! Check him!"

The freckled vigile reached under Longinus's tunic and blushed when he struck cock flesh far lower than it should be.

"Oh my."

"Pay his vulgar penis no mind!" Crassus was the stuff of nightmares. "Keep going until you reach the upper thigh."

The vigile looked at Longinus, who nodded. He felt for anything but only found more and more of the meaty appendage that dangled in the way.

"Nothing," he said.

"Here, let me!" Crassus reached up and then sneered at us both. "Check the boy." I had nothing to hide. The chamber pot was very close by and did not look right with a leather pouch inside. But the vigile paid close attention to me. I felt his hands graze my nearly non-existent genitals and jumped. He stood, sporting a tent-pole under his tunic.

"Here! Here it is!" Crassus pulled the shit-covered bag out of the chamber pot. "He's been robbing everyone on the Esquiline Hill."

There was no arguing around the several hundred aurei that spilled from the bag.

The vigile was unable to keep his erection from showing. I think he likes boys like me, with the small parts. He certainly showed no interest in Longinus and his mammoth cock.

The vigile spoke, "This is damning evidence. I have no choice but to throw you into prison. You have one minute to gather your belongings."

Porcius pleaded. "But sir, they are mine; they have done no wrong. They are fullers, not assassins! When will I have my property back?"

"They are going to the Tullianum, where they will be executed forthwith. We cannot compensate you. We advise you to keep a tighter rein over your slaves in the future."

As we were locked in chains, I heard Crassus snicker.

Longinus waited until we were moving to speak.

"I have the document of citizenship. I put it in my loincloth."

"Did you put any gold coins there, perhaps?"

He shook his head. "I have a plan."

"We're going to the dungeons under the Forum. They will behead us for murder. What can we do?"

"Once these chains come off, I can pose as a free man visiting you, my slave. They will let me leave."

"And you will leave me behind?"

"I put on this toga because you can hide beneath it."

"Longinus, the prison has been around for 800 years. Do you think they haven't seen such a trick?"

"Has anyone entering the prison had papers giving them free passage?"

I shrugged. "Thousands, no doubt."

The Tullianum was a judicial building with a vast complex of dungeons beneath. Our situation was hopeless.

Then a marvelous coincidence occurred. To reach the dungeons, you must pass through the courts. Slaves have no right to a trial, so the redheaded vigile whisked us through. But sitting on the magistrate's panel was Ursus! I called his name.

Ursus looked up at me and smiled, then frowned.

He addressed the vigile. "I must ask you, sir, with what crime have these two men been accused?"

"Oh, they're not men, your honor; they are slaves."

Ursus nodded.

"I require two slaves in my chambers. There was a terrible spill. The papers need drying, but I don't think I'll ever get out the stains on the tapestry."

"These two are murderers, sir. But they also happen to be launderers. What will it be?"

"Murderers?" Ursus looked at me. "This slender young thing is a murderer?"

"And a thief." He held the stinky satchel filled with gold coins.

"Where do those coins belong?"

"They go back to the treasury, sir. The victim has no relatives, and his debts are paid."

I could see a miller's wheel grinding away in the mind of Ursus. At last, he spoke.

"I would like you to remand these slaves to my custody for an hour. After that, you may lock them away."

I worried he planned to fuck me until I bleed and throw us both into the pit. But, of course, he was a good, kind man with something else in mind.

"Come, lads; we have only an hour to pull this off."

He beckoned us into his chamber.

"First, I don't care what you did. I don't want to know. It would be dangerous for you to tell me, understood?"

We nodded.

Longinus presented the document of free passage through the Empire.

"Oh, wonderful. Did you steal this too? Wait, don't tell me."

"Ursus, we don't want you to get in trouble."

He looked at Longinus. "I'm afraid you will have to hit me rather hard. I may be a bit older, but I can take it."

Longinus punched him in the eye.

"Oww!!! I didn't mean right now." He held his head until he regained his balance.

I watched his fat, fat cock swing under his toga. Tunics revealed a man, but togas were meant to cloak. Ursus was so thick and heavy not even the layers of toga could hide his bulging manhood. He was a daddy with a baby between his legs.

"Let's make it look like a struggle happened. Toss a few books and scatter some scrolls."

We made quick work of destroying his office.

Ursus peeked out the door. "He's not there. The vigile has taken a break. This is your chance. Remember, you attacked a magistrate, so things will be rough for a few days. Do you have anywhere you can lay low?"

"The Saturni," I said.

"Perfect. They will protect you. However, they live almost next door to a bloody murder scene. Awful, it happened last night. The poor man was disemboweled. The area will have many officials and vigiles, so use caution." He stopped and asked, "That wasn't you last night? Don't tell me!"

Longinus needed to get it off his chest. "I will say it's rare you find a man eviscerated with no knife wounds."

Ursus nodded. He knew far more than he wanted to.

In a show of pantomime, he shook Longinus's hand and patted me on the head, pretending to chit-chat. Then he pushed us both forward. We exited the building and walked through the forum.

"Longinus, it will be hard to get that money back."

He scowled. "It's gone. All those mouthfuls and ass-fuls of cum you took, and it's just gone. Vanished."

"So is our home and our freedom if we are captured."

19

HELP FROM FRIENDS

When we arrived at the Villa Saturni, we saw Otto bathing in the private garden. He started when he saw us.

"Longinus? Formosus? To what do I owe such unexpected pleasure?"

He stepped out of the bath and wrapped himself in a linen cloth. His snake-like appendage peeked out from under the fabric.

"Your neighbor Ursus suggested we seek refuge here."

"Refuge?"

"It's a long story; perhaps we can tell you inside."

After recounting our tale of woe, we drank a hot beverage made from toasted barley. Drusilla fussed over us while arranging the guest room.

Otto spoke, "We have servants, and servants talk. I only hope you were not overheard. The official story - you are a distant cousin and his slave."

I smiled weakly. This was kindness beyond all compare, but it made me worry for these friendly people who took in criminals. It made me stew in guilt, knowing I was indeed a criminal. It was a strange, self-inflicted crime; taking the money made it much worse. Had we taken our twenty, it would have been just, although leaving a shit-stained corpse for his slave to find was despicable at best.

I wanted to hate Longinus, but he had made life worthwhile these past few months. I knew he hadn't intended to plunge us into a netherworld of shadows and hiding, but here we were.

Drusilla was very direct. "I know they will come here asking what we saw. I have nowhere to hide you. Despite the size of the villa, it has few places that remain unexposed. I would go with the story of the cousin and slave, but it's very risky."

I looked at Longinus. He said, "Then we should leave immediately."

Otto held up a hand. "I don't know how you are connected to the murder of Abyssus Obediaens, but if it was you, I owe you a handsome reward. He was despicable, ready to sell his neighbors' dignity for a gold coin. So, since you couldn't tell me even if I asked, I will assume you deserve the reward."

He handed us a sack filled with Aurei and Denarii. It was a fraction of what we had lost, but it would be something.

"The Via Appia is heavily patrolled, but it is the fastest way out of town. I suggest you do something to disguise yourselves." Drusilla gave me a wig of long blond hair.

"Longinus, will you allow me to cut your locks short?"

He agreed. He looked ten times more handsome with a short haircut.

Otto had advice as well. "You mustn't rely on those papers for very long. If they are missing, the owner will have reported it. The further you get from Rome, the more useful they may become."

Longinus asked, "We are going near Capua. Which road must we take?"

"The Via Appia goes directly. If you can evade the

authorities, you may want to take a boat from Ostia. I recommend buying a horse and using the road. Turn into every town and take every trail that runs beside it. You will encounter fewer agents of Rome."

Drusilla asked, "Where are you going?"

"New City."

"Neapolis. You will be protected from the clutches of Rome, for now. Go quickly before your luck turns."

They sent us on a path leading straight to the Pyramid of Cestius at the Porta Ostiense. That road led to Ostia, the seaport. We skirted the walls by traveling past ramshackle homes along narrow alleys that surrounded the walls. We passed the Porta Ardeatina, which was overrun with legionaries, ready to turn back any non-Romans who dared to enter without proper documentation. They were not interested in a handsome Plebeian and his blond slave boy that wandered past.

At last, we reached the Appian Way. It was the pride of the Empire. The cobblestones were so perfectly aligned that a carriage of standard width could put its wheels in the ruts and never have to steer the horses. It ran in a perfectly straight line for miles. It was extremely busy. We walked two miles before I saw a welcome sight. It was the temple of Mars.

It was growing dark, and we needed somewhere to stay. I saw the priest Pius on the steps, brushing away leaves. The temple was white with a brilliant frieze in bold colors.

"Salve, Pius"

Gentlemen, hello! I wondered if you would take me up on the offer. It seems I am of good fortune. I must warn you; there are other members here that will probably want to get their swords wet. Are you up for the challenge?"

I wanted to sleep, but I nodded. "I take all comers."

"Dinner is in an hour. Perhaps we can get you a few appetizers before we sit."

Inside the temple of Mars, a colossus representing the God of war, military force, and, paradoxically, peace dominated the room. There were dozens of worshippers come to pay their respect or make an offering.

I looked around. The temple was completely exposed.

"Where will this feast take place?"

Pius laughed.

"We live in the building surrounding the temple. The entrance is beneath the colossus."

We descended a staircase to a locked door. The priest pulled out a large key and let us in. I worried that we might be entering a trap. Longinus squeezed my hand in the dimly lit passageway. I felt safe.

20

IN THE TEMPLE OF
MITHRAS

The stairs went down much deeper than expected. We were underground. A narrow tunnel led to a door with a raven engraved on the wood. Pius stepped back and let me open the door. I walked into a dimly lit chamber, where a man with grey curly locks sat nude on a wooden platform. As our eyes cleared, we realized he had a bow and arrow pointed at us.

"Ravens, bow down to your Pater."

Pius was not here. We were alone with our "Pater."

"Remove your garments." He kept the bow held back the whole time, ready to shoot whoever rushed him first. I removed my clothes and the strange blond wig Drusilla had given me.

"Sandals too."

We were stark naked, waiting to be executed.

"Do you renounce all worldly ties? Are you ready to be initiated in the Secrets of the East?"

I looked at Longinus. What possessions did we have but each other?

I spoke first. "I am keeping my clothing and my love for him."

Longinus had a better answer. "Even my clothing would mean nothing without Formosus."

The Pater released the arrow. It sailed between us, so close it blew air in my ear. It struck the stone wall behind us and stuck. Water cascaded from the newly made hole in the stone.

Longinus stood to rush the Pater and overpower him, but the room filled with cheering naked men, including Pius. We were clapped heartily on the back by handsome, swarthy men, and offered soft, whispered congratulations from thin, pretty men with round bottoms and tiny genitals like mine. Many appeared to be soldiers. Others were Plebeians or craftsmen. I may have spied one or two who appeared to be escaped slaves.

Longinus was far angrier than me. "What is the meaning of this bullshit!?"

Pius smiled. "You were just initiated into the Mithraeum. You couldn't be down here until we got that part worked out. You passed immediately, which is rare."

"Passed what?"

"Initiation."

I looked around the room. It was a vast assortment of men, all completely unclothed and eager to meet us both.

Pius continued, "The temple above is devoted to an old, outdated god, Mars. Mithras is the real god. He doesn't just create wars and give soldiers work. Mithras protects soldiers and brings good fortune to those who follow him. He escorts his devotees to a home in the sky when their lives on Earth end."

Longinus nodded. "He sounds great. Why the bow and arrows?"

"It's a simple test. We initiate two brothers at a time. If they each try to attain membership for only themselves, the arrow is put away, and they are sent home. If they show love and selflessness, the Pater shoots the water stone. If it remains dry, they are sent home. If it produces water, as Mithras wills it, they are accepted. So welcome!"

The Pater spoke. "Let us build our appetite for the feast."

Instantly, the room of naked men became a writhing orgy of the flesh. Cocks, butts, and mouths met, entered, kissed, swallowed, and penetrated. A strong soldier grabbed me by the waist and entered me. He was a big man in every way, but Longinus had made me loose. He fucked me hard, but I felt no pain or discomfort. I felt only pressure. His fucking was a warm vibration with an erotic effect on my tiny penis. I dribbled. Out of the corner of my eye, I saw two young men built much like me. They had both pressed their butts against the mighty cock of Longinus. Their cheeks encircled my protector's flesh pole. They rode up and down, causing him to thrash and moan.

My soldier pounded me like a hammer on steak. It felt good. To my surprise, I realized a second soldier had entered me from below. It felt good to be stretched wide. Longinus couldn't hold back. The double butt frottage must have felt good. He shot skyward. It rained sperm. I caught a drop on my tongue. It was intoxicating. I let soldier after soldier work their way in, leave a deposit, and exit quietly.

At last, I felt a familiar cock at my back door. Longinus had found me. He grabbed me around the waist and pulled me to a stone table. He lay me flat and pushed his way into me. I wrapped my legs around his waist and pulled him closer to me. At last, I felt satisfied.

Once Longinus was hip-to-ass with me, he took long, rough strokes. I moaned. The rest of the brotherhood formed a semi-circle around us, stroking themselves. I heard gasps as Longinus fucked deep, revealing the moving lump on my skin formed by his cockhead inside me, going deeper than man can go.

He kissed me deeply. As his tongue swabbed my tonsils, I licked back, causing his already massive cock to grow even thicker. The increased pressure made my small penis dribble the clear juice. When Longinus's fingers grew wet with my juice, he put them in his mouth.

His eyes closed. "Oh, Formosus, you taste so sweet."

His compliment only made me gush more. As he slurped his fingers, his cock grew thicker still. I felt my rectum dilate with the added pressure. Longinus pulled out all the way to show my gaping hole to the brotherhood. Astonished breaths told me my asshole was impressive.

One young man stepped forward and shot his semen into my open hole. Longinus used it as lubricant. He was mightily aroused, for he grew thicker and longer still.

Two more men stepped forward. Longinus withdrew. Both men hit the mark. They were soldiers with good aim. I felt the hot fluid seep into me through my stretched hole.

This continued until, at last, the Pater himself shot his load into my cavernous asshole. A river of semen filled me, and a bog of cum lay on my balls, perineum, buttocks, and thighs. While Longinus prepared the final load, I gathered the stray seeds in my fingers and gobbled them up. To taste so many men at once was ecstasy. Each handful had blends of flavors like garum, salt, grapes, sardines, shrimp, moss, mead, and honey. I writhed in uncontrollable orgasm and showered the brotherhood with my cum. Longinus held himself deep inside me. I felt his balls pump and his cock throb like a bee's stinger. Somewhere very far inside me, another tributary to the Sperm River was formed. Hot goopy strings of cum warmed my colon.

When Longinus pulled out, still rock hard, his cock

was soaked in the semen of the thirty men who had aimed and fired into my stretched asshole.

The thin, passive young men licked Longinus clean, a formidable task with their small tongues. The more masculine soldiers and tradesmen waited with a bowl. I expelled the thirty loads in peristaltic bursts. Last and deepest was the mega load of cum from Longinus. It was still hot and steamy and much thicker than the others.

The bowl was passed among the masculine men, including Longinus. There was still a lot left in the bowl when it was finally given to me. As I drank the mouthfuls of come, my eyes fluttered. I saw a vision of a lion-headed man wrapped in two thick snake-like cocks. I was drunk on semen. I lost consciousness.

When I came out of my reverie, Pius and Longinus were by my side in a dark room lit only by one candle.

Pius spoke first. "Are you well?"

"I feel better than ever."

Longinus sighed with relief. The last thing he wanted was to injure me with his tree trunk cock.

Pius asked, "What did you see?"

I frowned. "See?"

"It is common for initiates to have visions if they grow intoxicated from semen."

"I saw a lion-headed man."

Pius gasped. "Was he wrapped in snakes?"

I nodded. "They were cocks, not snakes. Longinus's cock, only two of them."

Pius produced a figurine of a lion-headed man wrapped in snakes. "You saw Arimanius. The cocks are the message."

"Why two?" Longinus was curious.

"Has Formosus grown down there?" I laughed, but when I looked, my cock, indeed, was slightly larger.

"Semen has magical properties, which is why it

brings on visions. It makes babies and can change your physical form for better or worse."

I was worried. "But will Longinus still want me? Longinus, do you wish me to remain small?"

Longinus smiled. "I would love you if your cock dragged behind you on the ground; I only hope your soft round buttocks don't change to a muscled pair like mine."

I checked my ass to see, and they both laughed.

"Still soft." But it had dimples on the sides that were never there before.

y eyes adjusted to the light. The men sat about naked in reclining poses on the banquettes that lined the stone table, where Longinus had opened me wide, allowing the men to fill me with their semen like they were tossing coins in a fountain.

"I saved two seats of honor for you."

The first soldier to fuck me asked, "Is our novice alright?"

Pius grinned, "Never better. He had a vision of Arimanius."

The table resounded with excited chatter.

"Does he know what gift he will be given?"

"Arimanius will give him a horse's cock to match his lover. It has already begun."

More chatter erupted as Pius lifted my tunic to show my slightly larger cock.

The food came in waves. We started with thinly sliced preserved bear served on unleavened bread with cheese. The bear came from Thrace.

The second wave was a crab soup and deep-fried oysters. We ate from spoons whose handles resembled snakes.

All of this was in preparation for the actual feast,

which was lamb in a wine and liquamen sauce. My closest seatmate told me it was not liquamen but kosher garum. Apparently, the Jews have a method of fermenting fish intestines that imparts a subtle flavor and does not cause vomiting or fever as lower-quality garum will do.

A greasy baked goose with Eastern spices and dried grapes followed the lamb. All of this was washed down with conditorium. After the third glass, I felt the glow, which grew stronger.

The feast ended with a giant platter of fruits and cheeses from around the Roman Empire. During dessert, I felt a hand squeeze my bottom. I leaned in the opposite direction, and the hand found my hole, still wet with semen. I was too lit up on the conditorium to care who it was. Besides, I needed all the sperm I could get.

I felt a large cockhead enter my hole, followed by a very long cock. When at last, the cock had plumbed my depths, I turned my head to see the Pater buried deep inside me. I obliged him.

The room had broken out into a new orgy. The fruits and cheeses that remained were staining the bottoms of the thin men who lay prostrate on the table, taking cock from all the brothers in turn.

Pater pushed me gently onto the fruit-filled table, and I became part of the anus chain. Cock after cock would penetrate me, some leaving semen, others moving to the next luscious bottom. One soldier grunted as he ate cherries from next to my head. I felt his semen pour into me. He pulled out and moved to the next boy, smacking his penis into his open palm to revive it.

I heard a scream at one end of the table. Cries of "No!" Or "I can't!" Longinus was making his way around.

At last, he came to me. He entered me quickly on a

slick riverbed of fresh cum. He picked me up off the table and laid me flat on the bench. He rolled my legs above my head so my hole was at waist level.

"Fuck me. Hard."

Longinus whipped in and out of me at breathtaking speed. I needed more and more of his huge cock and delicious, magical cum. I wanted to be big like him.

My anal canal was worn from all the fucking I endured that day, but Longinus was like an ointment or balm to soothe the pain. Most of the men were impressive in different ways, but only a few could go into the deepest part where Longinus always went. None could go all the way to the place where his cock protruded from my belly; only Longinus had the right tool for that job.

I was the only one with the right-shaped hole for him. He never hurt me, and I had no injuries. We were a perfect match. If we were citizens and not slaves, I might ask to be married. Just being with him, even as a fugitive, was enough.

I felt his cum release in my guts. He took an empty glass and caught every drop that spilled from me while he withdrew. He held out his monstrous cock for me to clean. I did it slowly, lovingly, and with great attention. I loved his cock. Just looking at it gave me an instant erection. I looked down and saw mine was just a bit larger than the last time I checked. I downed the glass of cum like a man drinks water at a desert oasis. Longinus ate cheese, cherries, grapes, and other fruits from my backside.

Pius escorted us to the guest wing, where we shared a room with two small cots.

In the morning, we would tell him our plight and ask for his help with our escape from Rome.

❧ 22 ❧
NEW GROWTH

Pius was upset by our story. He, too, knew Abyssus and thought him wretched, but couldn't see him deserving to die at the hands, nay, the cock of Longinus.

"He had more enemies than allies, but powerful people will place a bounty on your head. They will fear you may know things."

Longinus asked, "I consider you a friend and ally. As such, I will not place you in jeopardy."

"You are a novice, but you have the protection of the Mithraic Brotherhood. Still, the greater part of the semen spilled last night belonged to mercenaries. We are a new sect. You mustn't trust anyone else with this."

I spoke. "The official story is that Longinus is my master. We are traveling to Neapolis to live as a couple in the manner of the Greeks."

Prius smiled. "Excellent. That is a story worth telling. The Christ himself would approve."

I had heard legends of the man called the Son of God, or Christ. The many who secretly met in his honor were persecuted. They were a threat to the Imperial cult. Nero spread lies that they were the ones who set fire to Rome nearly 25 years ago. Pius knew

Christ would approve because He said that love is the only law before the Hebrew God.

Pius continued, "We allow Christians to gather here in secret. The love brotherhood is a friend to Mithras."

"Do they feast and have orgies?"

Pius laughed. "I have no idea. We close the doors."

The Appian Way was the most direct route to Capua and the road to Neapolis. Along the road were towns. And patrolling the highways were Roman soldiers. Our document and thin disguises would be our only defense against bounty collectors.

"In the town of Terracina, there is a brother, Procerus Mentulum, who will give you sanctuary underneath his inn if you give the handshake."

Pius quickly taught us the unusual two-finger clasp that let the followers of Mithra identify themselves in secret.

"Once safely underground, you will tell him you are two novices headed for the Neapolis. He will ensure your safety within the town.

"There are Christians in Capua. They know our handshake. Use it only if you are in danger. The house is on the central piazza. You will know it for the small wooden cross carved on the lintel. There is a secret chamber beneath the building. Your handshake will be your key."

After Capua, it would be only a day's walk or a short horse ride down the Via Atellana to the Neapolitan port.

It was early in the day, but Pius thought it best we begin under cover of darkness.

One of the brothers loaned us his horse for as far as Terracina. After that, we would be on foot.

When I went to piss out the alcohol from last night's feast, I was stunned. My penis looked strange; it was no longer small. I stroked it and watched it reach a size that would allow penetration; it was as long as my thumb. I ran to tell Longinus the news.

"Let me see."

He kneeled to lift my tunic. I was still excited. Longinus sucked on my new, larger cock. I had never felt someone's lips sliding up and down my shaft. I couldn't hold back and squirted a huge amount of cum in Longinus's mouth. He kissed me, sharing my seed. I could almost feel my penis grow.

I returned the favor, taking all of Longinus and greedily hoarding his semen all to myself. I kissed him, but the sperm had bypassed my mouth and went straight down the esophagus.

"You're greedy, aren't you?"

I smiled. "I have a lot of catching up to do."

23

FIRST TIME

After the moon set, we rode out of the outskirts of Rome on our shared horse. I sat behind Longinus, wrapping my arms around his waist and stroking his nipples under the toga. I saw the fabric rise, and my tunic rose in response. To my astonishment, Longinus leaned forward and said, "Fuck me."

My cock nearly exploded just hearing those words. I found my way under the folds to the brown winking eye. After distributing my saliva, I shifted forward and entered Longinus in a single thrust.

"Ow! Shit!"

I had no sympathy, for I had endured much, much more with no pain at all. To imagine my little penis hurting him was laughable.

Soon, the sharp intakes of breath and groans of pain melted into sighs and moans of pleasure. I never dreamed I would be able to do this with him. I rocked my hips in the rhythm that had always felt best inside of me. The horse's trot only served to enhance the pleasures we both felt.

"Oh, Formosus, that feels so fucking good."

"I know." It was unlike any sex I had ever known. My cock was inside the man I loved, and he was enjoying it. Thank Mithras for miracles.

As the horse trotted, adding to our pleasure, I reached around and wrapped my fingers partway around Longinus's shaft. Rubbing up and down, I held onto his waist with my other hand. I couldn't take long strokes, but I could make him feel good.

My smaller cock was the first to come. I shot my first load ever inside a man's ass. And that man, my love, was close, too.

Longinus leaned to one side so that I could suck the head of his cock. I didn't spill a drop when he came in my mouth. We kissed and shared his musky-scented seed that tasted of fresh butter and anchovies.

He used the stirrups to lift himself. I buried my face in his anus. He farted my come into my mouth. Another kiss, and we had shared breakfast.

I looked under my tunic and saw my cock was plump. My penis had grown past my balls. It touched the horse's back!

❧ 24 ❧

SEX MAGIC

Our horse grew tired, and darkness fell, so we walked. Away from the sodden floors of the fullonica, my feet cracked and blistered. Longinus had only worked a few months in the Orinari. He wasn't fragile, either. His feet were just fine in their sandals. As the sun rose, I couldn't hide my flayed feet from him.

"Does this hurt?" He asked, taking one foot in his hand.

I winced. "Yes."

"There's some mint; let's stop."

After finding two retired paving stones, Longinus put stems of mint on the stone and crushed it. He tipped the stone to gather the essence in a clay bowl. When the bowl was half full, he poured small amounts into his cupped hand and rubbed it on the cracks and leaves of skin. It helped. When all the mint had been applied, he took some fresh stems and wove them through my sandals like bandages.

"Do you feel better?" He kissed my feet.

"Yes, but we have lost time."

"To take away your pain is no loss of time, Formosus. And now we can gallop for a while to make up time."

"Galloping will attract attention."

We continued at a trot until we reached the suburb called Aricia. As the first town after Rome, the citizens saw hundreds of travelers. They paid us no mind. We were able to buy some bread and cheese for our lunch. We overheard talk of 'two slaves who had murdered their master's client.' That wasn't good.

Longinus dared fate. "Salve," he spoke to one of the gossips. "I hear talk of murder. Should we be careful on the road?"

"Oh yes. They say this road may be their route of escape."

"How shall we know them?"

"I don't know."

That was a relief to hear. Nobody knew what we looked like. My blond wig may not have even been necessary, but it was better to be safe than sorry.

We rode out of Aricia reassured. We saw very few passengers on the road. It was summer, and travel was hard on horses and passengers alike. We were overtaken and passed by a black horse with a Roman rider, who traveled at full gallop. I felt sorry for him and his horse. I was grateful he didn't stop and question us.

As the shadows grew long, we reached the outskirts of Terracina, called Anxur by the Etruscans who founded the ancient seaport.

There was a military checkpoint with several guards. We could not avoid it, so we held our heads high and stopped.

"Please dismount." The guard was not friendly. "Do you have papers?"

I sighed with relief.

Longinus presented the travel document. The guard nodded. "Where is his?"

"He is my property. I need no papers."

"He is well-dressed for a slave."

"I take good care of my property, sir."

The guard smiled. I noticed the black horse that passed us. The soldier had stopped here at the mutationes and traded for a new horse. It left me uneasy.

One soldier consulted a scroll. He stepped forward.

"There are two murderers on the loose. We just received descriptions, and our orders are to check all male travelers."

Longinus blushed. "I don't understand."

"I apologize, but I must ask you to lift your toga. And tell your slave to lift his tunic."

Longinus raised the cloth covering his massive cock and giant balls. The look on the soldier's face was comical, but his actions were not.

"Got one!"

They threw a net over Longinus, quickly subduing him with a sharp trident.

Meanwhile, another soldier felt my average penis and shook his head.

"Doesn't match the description."

I cast a glance at the scroll and saw the words "extremely large cock," and "almost nonexistent penis." Perhaps most infuriating were the words "according to Crassus Commodus, the house slave."

One soldier said, "The boy may be an accomplice."

Longinus cried through the net, "We met on the road. He asked me for a ride. He has nothing to do with it."

A guard roared at me, "Is this true?"

I nodded. "I was so surprised when he declared me his property. I didn't know what to say."

The other guard asked, "Why are you on the Via Appia?"

I smiled. "I visited my cousins in Aricia. I'm staying at the inn belonging to Procerus Mentula."

"Where is your home?"

"Capua."

They waved me on.

"I can't believe I hitched a ride with a murderer! I hope he's going straight to Rome."

The guard liked my looks. He shook his head. "Maybe tomorrow. Tonight he will be held in the Tullianum next to Procerus's inn. You should be safe; that jail is guarded and secure."

As soon as I was out of sight, I burst into tears. I waited to regain my composure and then marched to the waterfront. I found the inn by hiding and then following at a great distance as they marched Longinus to the Tullianum. The inn was next door, just as they told me.

Inside, a tall friendly gentleman was rinsing cups.

"Evening. What can I do for you?"

"Is Procerus here?"

"He is." The man wiped his hands and came out from behind the counter. "I am he."

I extended a hand and grasped his wrist with two fingers.

"Come on." He escorted me back to the kitchen and opened a trap door.

Silently, we descended to a palatial underground temple.

"Son, you look like you've been crying."

I nodded.

"Well, out with it, then."

I told him everything. As the tale became more twisted, he winced.

"So the love of your life and fellow escaped murderer slave is in the Tullianum?"

I nodded.

"Well, thank Mithras, you're a novice. My job is to help in whatever way I can."

"I don't think you can help."

Procerus folded his arms. "Your lack of faith is troubling, brother. We are everywhere."

He put an arm around me. It was not meant to be

sexual, but I made it so. I stood on the tips of my toes and kissed him. He met my kiss.

I couldn't believe what a betrayal this seemed.

"Procerus, I'm so worried, and I shouldn't be doing this."

"We can do nothing for your beloved until we invoke Mithras through sex magic."

"Sex magic?"

"Hasn't something magic happened to you since initiation?"

I thought about my dick. I nodded.

"That energy will be needed to work a miracle for Longinus, you see?"

He poured some fortified wine for us both.

And so the orgy of two began.

The name Procerus means "towering." I assumed it referred to his taller-than-average build. I was wrong.

I lifted my tunic. Procerus dropped his toga. His cock was nearly identical to Longinus's but perhaps a pollex or two shorter. He turned and sighed.

"It may be best if you fuck me," he said, "I don't want to hurt you."

I laughed. You and Longinus could be twins.

He needed no further persuading. I felt the delicious sensation of his giant cockhead poke its way through me and into my shitter. I moaned with pleasure as Procerus hit the back wall. He began rocking his hips, sliding back and forth. Half his cock was out in the open air.

"Procerus, go all the way."

"But that's as far as it goes."

I held his buttocks and twisted as I pressed him into me. He turned the corner and gasped as I engulfed his cock with my innards.

"Did I tear a hole in you?"

"Shut up and fuck me harder."

We rutted like farm animals. I grunted like a hog. He whinnied like the horse he was.

My insides became tingly as they had done with Longinus.

Procerus said, "Do you feel that tingling? That's the magic! Keep going."

I was always focused on the end when orgasm brought relief, but Procerus showed me how to keep the magic going for a long time. He insisted we go until the tingling was unbearable, then go some more.

"It takes a lot of magic to bust an accused murderer out of jail."

Everywhere his cock came in contact with my guts was like a flint striking stone. The fire was magic. I could taste and see it, like a blue billowing cloud of smoke.

"Now, Formosus, when we finally move beyond this delicious torture and release our seed, you must focus all your energy on the outcome you want. Put the thoughts into the blue smoke and let them become one."

"Yes. Yes. Oh yes, I will." And with that, I rubbed Procerus's nipples while thinking about a beautiful home in Neapolis with Longinus. My new, bigger cock spewed cum on everything and everyone. It didn't come in droplets...it was thick and hot like Longinus.

Procerus came on the out stroke. The semen met my tingling guts and set them ablaze with magic. I saw my cock grow visibly before my eyes. The blue smoke wound in a cyclone, then billowed out of the underground temple.

"Where did it go?"

"It's going to the jail. Come on, get dressed."

When we arrived at the jail, the moon was setting. I don't know how many hours Procerus fucked me, but it was more than I had imagined.

The door to the jail was open, and both guards were asleep.

I saw blue smoke hovering over their nostrils.

I removed a set of keys from the guard's belt and found the cell where Longinus slept. He woke when I gently shook him.

"Formosus. I must be dreaming" He embraced me.

Procerus motioned us to leave. Longinus arranged the blanket to appear like a sleeping man. I locked the cell and put the keys back on the belt of the sleeping guard.

Outside the jail, Procerus pointed to a blue cloud moving towards the waterfront.

On the beach, fishermen were preparing their nets. The blue cloud surrounded an old man who was ready to sail.

Procerus spoke. "Salve, Bruno. Can you give these friends a ride to Neapolis?"

"No, it's too far. But I can take them as far as Sinuessa. Come on." As he reached out an arm to pull me aboard, I felt two fingers around my wrist. I returned the secret handshake, and he smiled at me. "Oh, son, I hope you need magic." He patted my bottom.

I gave Procerus a long kiss goodbye.

"I meant to ask you, what magic did you receive as a novice?"

"Same as you." He grabbed his giant meat under his toga. "I was tiny. I'll bet you were too."

Out on the open sea, we were safe. No doubt there was pandemonium on land in the wake of our escape. I treasured the peace of the water.

While we helped Bruno pull in the nets, Longinus asked, "What were you and Procerus talking about?"

"Mithras bestows magic on his followers. We used it to break you out of jail and to find Bruno.

The fisherman smiled. "Your smoke is such a brilliant blue; I have seen nothing like it."

"What color is yours, Bruno?"

"It is a brown-green, the color of seaweed."

Longinus looked more confused than ever.

"What magic did Mithras give you?"

At that moment, the nets came to the surface. We tugged with all our strength, and a massive catch of giant mullet landed in the flat bottom of the hull. Bruno pointed, "Fish magic."

"What are you guys talking about?" Longinus gave an exasperated sigh.

I said, "It's hard to explain."

Bruno contradicted me. "Nonsense! It's really quite simple. It's just hard to believe."

"It? What's 'it'?"

I took a deep breath. "Magic. Do you remember the arrow that struck water from stone? That was magic."

Longinus nodded.

"My tiny penis is grown to normal size; that's magic."

I felt worried about the next confession. "In order to rescue you, Procerus and I generated a powerful cloud of magic."

Bruno interrupted. "You did that with Procerus? You poor sweet boy. I'm surprised you can walk!"

Before Longinus could twist our selfless act into something indecent, I explained. "It's sex magic. It can only be summoned through sex. The sex must last a long time for it to gain power. That's all I know."

Bruno filled in some gaps. "It must be sex between men. The most powerful is Greek sex. Oral sex can only influence, but doesn't change matter."

I added, "Every time you fuck me, my dick grows. That was Mithras' gift to me."

I kissed Longinus. He had a lot to digest.

"So, you let Procerus fuck you?"

"To break you out of jail."

"You barely knew him, Formosus."

"We barely knew anyone we fucked in the temple." His jealousy was frustrating. "And he taught me how to make it powerful by delaying."

Bruno wiped his forehead. "You did that with Procerus? How are you even standing?"

I wrapped my hands around the base of Longinus's mighty cock and lifted it skyward. "I had a lot of practice, Bruno."

The old fisherman whistled. "This was not magic; it was the blessing of Mithras at birth."

Longinus nodded. "Mixed blessing."

Bruno turned to me. Blessing or curse?"

"I can't get enough. Our journey started with his big dick, and some of our worst troubles were due to the beautiful monster. But we are at sea with you, and the troubles remain on shore. If I look at the big picture, it is certainly a blessing. And if I take a selfish view, my body cavity craves him with a desire no other man, not even Procerus, can fulfill. That we found each other is the greatest blessing of all."

"Come here, little man." Longinus caught me around the waist and sat me in his lap. I felt him growing hard beneath me.

Bruno rubbed his crotch staring at me with longing. He said, "We need a lot of sex magic to get you out of Sinuessa. We have no brethren there, and it is an outpost for the legionaries."

"Should you drop us off instead at Minturnae? It's closer."

"No, your best chance is to come ashore as a fisherman. There is no way to hide that log of flesh, but carrying my trawling net in need of repair to the retificium will be an excellent disguise. A temple dedicated to Minerva is a few doors further up the hill. Wait there, praying, and we will come for you after I have sold my catch."

Longinus said, "Fine. Now how does sex magic work?"

Bruno released his short fat cock and put it against my lips. As I leaned forward to put it in, Longinus held me aloft and set me down on his cock. I worried it would be sore from all I had done with Procerus, but it was better than ever before. I immediately began tingling and closed my eyes, picturing the tingling passing from me to him.

"Whoa," said Longinus, "What was that?"

I took Bruno out of my mouth and answered, "Magic."

Bruno proved challenging. His cock was as big around as it was long. My mouth knew how to take a long thick cock, but short ones were not as easy.

Longinus got to his knees so his deep thrusts did not have to fight gravity. I spread my legs apart and held the butt cheeks open to give him unfettered access to my twitching hot hole.

When Bruno fell out of my mouth for the fifth time, I gave Longinus instructions.

"Your goal is to make this tingling continue until sundown."

"That's many hours from now!"

"If magic were easy, everyone would do it."

Bruno pumped himself in my mouth with short strokes. I did not need to take him down my throat. In fact, I could not.

Bruno asked Longinus, "What magic did Mithras give you?"

"Formosus is growing a cock like mine. He was tiny."

Bruno chuckled. "That's not your magic. He gave you something special. It is that which you desire most in this world."

"No, nothing."

"So, nothing unexplainable or magical has happened?"

Longinus shook his head. Then, "Oh wait!" He produced his coin purse from under his toga.

"At first, I thought I was bad at counting. Then I decided Pius had put these in as a parting gift."

He took out one gold coin, then two, then a dozen.

Bruno exclaimed, "Gold magic!" Oh, to be rich and have a big dick. You will both have good lives."

We fell silent for a while, focusing on the tingling and keeping it going. A long time passed, then Longinus began to take deep breaths. It was a sound he always made near climax.

I felt tingling in my mouth. Bruno was reclined on a pile of nets, smiling. I pinched him. He saw what was about to come.

"Oh! Longinus," the old fisherman said, "Has your gold doubled, or is it just a few coins?"

"I'm not sure." He checked his purse.

Bruno had successfully distracted Longinus from the brink of release. I myself was ready to explode, but I kept it contained. The shadows grew longer. We were all struggling not to go over the brink. Between my face and Bruno's crotch, a cloud of orange smoke formed and grew.

Behind me, a royal purple cloud rose into the sky. The longer we fucked, the bigger the cloud grew until it was bigger than the boat. The orange cloud met the purple and was subsumed, forming pools of orange in geometric patterns against the purple. We kept fucking and sucking until twilight. As the sun touched the horizon, we could hold it no longer.

Bruno came in my mouth, his legs quaking. I held him by the buttocks to keep him upright. He completely occupied my mouth. I swallowed what I could with my jaws stretched so far. The rest squirted out the sides of my mouth, landing on the fish. I held the heavy fat cock when I released it to lick it clean. Bruno ran his thick fingers through my hair.

Behind me, the purple cloud trailed the boat. In front, it was blowing toward shore.

Longinus let out a yell. "Fuck, Formosus, I can't hold back any more!!"

I rolled over onto my back so he was facing me. I kissed him. The tingling in our lips was a bolt of lightning that added to the all-over vibrations. This was it. Longinus touched my nipple, and my aching cock shot a massive arc of cum that hit me in the face. Longinus shook with unfulfilled desire. He licked my cum from my forehead and lips. "Oh shit, I'm coming!"

Longinus trembled so hard the boat rocked. "Oooh. Fuck. Ooh."

"Shoot it in me." I held his waist close while he bucked and writhed. Then it came. First, the familiar throbbing at the base began. Seconds later, a thick, syrupy ocean of cum flowed from his deeply implanted cock. His balls lifted over and over again, pumping so many times I lost count. Longinus had never come so hard and so much. I rubbed his nipples to keep the pump flowing. He spasmed and kept coming. The purple smoke surrounded us and filled our lungs. I could see nothing besides Longinus buried deep inside me. He stayed in me, gently pumping smaller and smaller loads. I felt full and satisfied. Longinus bent to kiss me, and I grew hard again. Now my cock was longer than Bruno's, and its circumference had increased. Longinus rubbed it for me, and when I unloaded a second time, he wrapped his mouth around it so he didn't miss a drop. I felt him swell inside me. He pummeled me again with an urgency brought on by the approaching shore. I twisted his nipples hard, and he released another raging flood of his sperm inside me.

There were no dishes, but Bruno gave us a clean pail. As Longinus withdrew, my body forcefully expelled ounce upon ounce of Longinus's seed. The bucket was nearly a quarter full when, at last, my ass had emptied itself.,

Longinus fed me his semen in small gulps. When I took a break, he fed himself. We were done just as the sun disappeared into the sea, and Bruno's boat landed on the sand at Sinuessa. Longinus hoisted Bruno's net over one shoulder and made his way to the rectificium, where they mended holes. The net did much to cover his manhood.

Bruno and I went to the fishmongers to sell his valuable catch of mullet. When we were done, we met up with Longinus in the temple of Minerva.

We were alone.

"To test how powerfully your magic worked, you must check your gifts."

I looked under my tunic to see what could only be called "a nice big dick." Longinus held his pouch of gold. It was more than twice its size.

Bruno smiled. "You will feel its presence throughout your life, but especially in the next few days. Sex magic at sea between lovers is one hundred times more potent than the magic you raised with Procerus."

We said our goodbyes and thanked Bruno for his guidance and protection.

I asked, "You did so much. How can we repay you?"

Bruno smiled. "The orange magic stayed over the water. Tomorrow I will catch enough mullet to retire. But if you wish to pay back my kindness further, you must show kindness to other brothers in the future."

PIGGY-BACK

To leave town, we had to cross a bridge patrolled by Legionaries. There was no avoiding it, so we crossed. At the far end, a Legionary asked for our papers. Then he said, "Formosus?" It was Claudius, the Legionary with whom I was first bold enough to give my name after cleaning his cock.

"Salve, Claudius."

"You are far from the fullonica!"

"I am."

Claudius said, "We're looking for a murderer. The thing is, he was caught up the road in Terracina. He vanished without a trace."

I asked, "Are we in danger?"

"Who is your friend?"

I said, "He is a deaf-mute. He's going to the Academy in Capua."

Claudius appeared puzzled. "There is a school for the deaf there?"

I said, "Christians run it."

"Sounds like something they would do. Buying indulgences so their God will show favor in the afterlife."

I shrugged. "It could be worse. Caring for the needy is pretty useful."

Claudius smiled. "You make a good point. By Mars,

he's hung like a horse!" He took a step backward as if Longinus's cock were a deadly viper.

"Most deaf people are," I lied, "The gods take away above but show favor below."

I was grateful I wasn't yet big enough to show under my tunic. There would have been far too many questions.

"Claudius, will we need protection on the road to Capua? Is there a murderer on the loose?"

"Impossible; he would have to get through two checkpoints and this one to be on that stretch of road. Far more likely, he has returned to Rome. I can promise you will be safe from here to Capua."

We kissed as old friends do, and I patted his crotch. "Still nice and long where it counts, Claudius."

He said, "Had I more time, I would prove it to you."

I grinned. "Oh, your training was all the proof I need."

"Your throat is a retreat from the cares of the world. Were I not working, I would have you now."

"I will visit on the way back." It was a falsehood, but one that saved precious time.

He grew concerned. "Capua is more than a day's walk from here. Do you have water?"

I shook my head. Claudius got a bottle made from sheep's bladder out of his tent.

"This will last the journey if you take small sips."

I asked, "Are there no towns or rivers ahead?"

"No, this stretch of the Appian is the least populated. You're lucky I gave you that!"

"So, it will be more than a day?"

He stroked his beard. "If you left in the morning, you would arrive when the moon was high. Since you're leaving when the moon is high, you should arrive in Capua by sundown tomorrow."

I kissed Claudius again, and we began our march inland toward Capua. We crossed out of Latium into

Campania. The Roman influence was strong nearly everywhere but more in Latium than anywhere else in the world. We were a tiny bit safer.

Walking at night was difficult. We had no candles, and the moon was but a thin crescent.

At sunrise, we shared some preserved fish that Bruno gave me. It was salty; we needed an extra helping of water. We passed fruit trees growing wild. We prepared a lunch of apples and cherries with a slice of cheese I had left from our journey's start.

The mile marker said we were 11 miles from Sinuessa and 19 miles from Capua. My feet began bleeding again. There was no mint here. Longinus put me on his shoulders. My cock rubbed against his neck. I felt it grow under my tunic until it poked past Longinus's ears. He easily turned his head and sucked on it like a baby nursing. There was so much more I could do with a big dick. Getting blown while riding on the shoulders of a handsome Thracian was just one of many things I wanted to do.

We both smelled rotten eggs. There was a sulfur spring nearby. We wandered off the road until we found it. The water was hot. It was surrounded by mud. Longinus told me to walk into the water. I did, and instantly my feet felt better. The long flakes of skin dissolved, leaving clean pink flesh. The warm mud was an excellent poultice. We wrapped my feet in wet strips of toga cloth to keep the soft earth in place. It was more magic at work.

I rode a few more miles on his shoulders until we reached the halfway mark. We were thirsty. The sheep bladder was less than half full. We drank in tiny sips to make it seem like more.

We were in midsummer. The heat was dangerous, so we rested in the shade of some oak trees. Longinus had gathered some of the sulphuric mud. He removed my dressings and applied fresh mud, wrapping it all back in cloth.

As Longinus bent to lace a sandal, I put my head under his toga and tongued his hole.

He kneeled to make it easier for me to fill his anus with slick saliva. He spread his knees wide so that his cock spread out on the ground. I squeezed his thick member and tugged like it was an udder. He wriggled and sighed. Who was I? A few days ago, I could never dream of what I would do next. I wet my dick with spit and penetrated Longinus.

He shrieked in pain. Again, I was hurting him, only more so. Me, Formosus, mouse-meat! I retreated but did not pull out. This technique has always worked for me. I felt a gentle release in the anus, so I plowed forward. I hit the back wall of the rectum. I didn't quite have the length to go deeper, so I contented myself by pushing hard against the rear wall.

"Oh, Formosus, you are so much bigger! You're going to split me in two!

Was he serious? I looked down at my cock, stretching Longinus open. I could scarcely believe how big the hole remained when I pulled out. I could spit in it, so I did.

I fucked him harder, pounding against his rear wall. He groaned with pain and moaned with pleasure.

I pulled out and saw him gape wide open again.

"Piss in me." Longinus was crazed with lust.

I put my cock back inside him.

"No, piss in my stretched hole." He spread his cheeks and offered his open hole to me.

It was so bizarre, and it made me even harder to think about it. Still, I managed to take a leak into his wide-open asshole. When his body began squeezing it out, I plugged the whole and finished my long piss. I kept fucking Longinus hard with all that urine in his belly. The spasms and contractions felt great on my dick.

He begged me to let him evacuate, but I was drunk on power over my protector. I fucked harder, and piss began to escape around my cock. I moved to one side and unplugged the hole. A river of piss and shit flew out of his ass and landed in the grass.

"I'm clean now," he said, "don't stop fucking me."

I put my dick back in. No magic had appeared; we would need a few hours for that.

We had to get moving, but I wanted to come inside Longinus. He had a brilliant idea.

He carried me on his back instead of his shoulders, holding my legs at the best angle to plunge in and out of him with each step.

Several parties bound for Rome passed us, and none suspected us of buggery. A few women gasped at the massive hardon Longinus kept covered with a toga, but they would never have imagined I was deep inside him. In this manner, we raised a purple cloud of sex magic. I heard coins fall into the pouch, and Longinus felt me turn the corner for the first time.

We knew it was time to finish when the cloud was high enough to catch a breeze. We turned off the road into a grove of cypress. Longinus lay on his back, looking up at me with the same helpless eyes I would use to look at him.

"Keep fucking me, Formosus; I'm ready to come."

I didn't want to miss a drop, so I put the head of his cock in my mouth while I pounded with abandon.

Longinus thrashed and blew out great gusts of air. My thick cock caused enough pressure to squeeze out drops of the clear sticky fluid that tasted like mussels. I kept sucking until I finally saw his balls retract, and the vein running the length of his fat cock began pulsing. I feasted on his cum. I was so into the moment that I didn't realize I was coming until it washed over me. My hips pressed tight against the Thracian's perfect buttocks. He contracted as he came in mouthfuls. The contractions squeezed more and more cum out of my cock. I sucked Longinus dry.

When I pulled out, Longinus farted my come into his palm, ate, then farted some more. I was amazed at how thick and white my cum was. Before magic, it was watery and grey.

❧ 26 ❧

MAXIMUS

With a purple cloud leading the way, we walked the last few miles to Capua. The sunset over the bay was a deep purple. I knew we had created that with our fucking.

The primary portal into the city was heavily guarded. The handsome guards were friendly and talkative. I used my charm to gather intelligence while Longinus held back. I would signal him to come by tossing my fake blond hair. I would scratch an insect bite if I felt he should stay back.

"Salve, pulchrae." Calling the guards handsome seemed an excellent way to start.

"Salve, pulchra." A particularly virile soldier returned the compliment using the feminine form. I dare not flirt too hard with these men, friendly or not.

"I've just come from Formiae." That was a town we had skipped by sailing.

The flirtatious, virile guard came close to me. "Your feet speak the truth, brother." He had a beard, a big hairy barrel chest, and tree trunk legs under his tunic.

I smiled. "They told me of two murderers on the road. I'm so glad I made it here alive!"

My bearded suitor put his arm around my waist. "Next time, ask one of us to escort you." He pulled me towards him. My skin brushed his thigh and smacked into a stiff, dangling knife.

"Is it safe to wear such a big knife under there?"

He shook his head. "It isn't."

"Isn't safe?" I felt a slight panic.

"Isn't a knife." He winked.

The whole regiment was laughing, but it was playful, not mean. This was taking longer than I expected.

"Did they catch the murderers?"

"Whoever put the bounty dropped it. Apparently, they murdered a friend of Vespasian but an enemy of Titus, the new Emperor. If anything, they are probably in his protection now with a handsome reward."

New Emperor? So much had happened in just a short time. It meant we were no longer fugitives. I tossed my blond hair, awaiting Longinus's approach.

But the barrel-chested guard with no knife took my hair flip as a flirtation."

He told the guards, "I'm taking this one to the barracks."

He picked me up and threw me over his shoulder. Now I would have to find a way to meet up with Longinus in this huge city; I couldn't anger this man. I kept chatting. "What is your name, soldier boy?"

"Maximus. And yes, it's because of my size."

"Your hairy chest and legs are enormous."

"That's not what I meant."

It felt bizarre to be carried like a sack of grain by this man. He was so broad that my waist fit easily on one shoulder.

"I understand."

"Have you played with the big boys? Do you like it to stretch you?" He asked.

"Yes, to both."

Maximus lifted my tunic and put a tongue on my hole. It was still sloppy from Longinus's recent invasion.

He licked up the remnants and grinned. "You've already had a visitor today."

"There's always room for more."

"Boy, I am gonna fuck that sloppy loose hole until it splits. You have never had anything like me."

Given how experienced and confident he was, I knew it was enormous, but not like my man's.

It seemed wise to encourage him.

"Oh no, Max, will it hurt?"

"It will tear you in two. You won't hear your farts for a week."

God, I hated how sexy he was. I forgot how big I had gotten until I felt it rubbing on Maximus's teat.

"Is that you, boy?" He turned me upside down, so my tunic fell over my eyes. "Fucking Mars, that's a big cock!" He was astounded. I didn't look like the type, and until recently, I wasn't.

"Yours is much bigger, I'm sure."

He grinned at the compliment. "Longer and thicker!"

We arrived at the barracks. His regiment was at the city gate, so his barracks were dark and empty.

"This is my bed."

As he tossed me gently on my back, I was shocked at how far I would go to ensure our safety. Longinus would do the same if the tables were turned. Right?

As I watched Maximus undo his belt and sword, I felt guilty. But my dick was standing straight up in the air. I was enjoying myself—time for some sex magic.

He dropped the red tunic, revealing a plump, swollen sausage about as long as my wrist to my elbow—a palm and foot, but not a cubit like Longinus. I greedily gulped down the stiff meat, keeping it deep in my esophagus for as long as I could, two short breaths, and right back down. A faint red cloud of dust stirred in the still room.

As I held on to Maximus, I got a thrill from the

muscles in his gigantic thighs. They dwarfed his big round balls that swayed gently, tapping my chin. More red dust.

"Son, you are one fine cocksucker. But I want into your ass."

I pulled away, leaving his cock dripping with throat juices. Maximus pressed against my opening, which yielded to the thick, powerful cock. He slid in and hit the wall. Try as I might, I could not get his rock-hard cock to turn the corner, so he pounded me hard in that painful place.

More red dust floated up and away from us. Maximus was too focused on my bottom to see it. The more painful it got, the more dust blew gently out of the windows into the night air. At last, something gave way, and he slipped further inside me. His eyes bulged.

"Did I hurt you?"

"On the contrary, you made it feel much better."

I looked at my dick towering in the air, with those powerful thighs of Maximus framing it. His broad chest cried out for touching. I rubbed his nipples. I may as well have set fire to him.

The thighs pushed hard and fast, smacking into my butt like an out-of-control chariot. He pounded, pounded, pounded while I rubbed his nipples. My head bumped rapidly against the wall. In a flash, Maximus ejected his seed into my bottom. Red dust was so thick I could barely see him. He did not comment on the cloud; perhaps only I could see it.

He looked down at my cock and shook his head. "My eyes are playing tricks. Your dick is bigger still and swelling."

I looked at the growing penis and shrugged.

Maximus leaned in and whispered, "Your turn now."

To my surprise, the giant bear of a man lay on his back and split those massive legs, putting a knee to each ear. A hairy asshole winked hungrily at me.

He reached behind him and grabbed a tiny clay crock containing grease; he rubbed the ointment inside his hole.

"Come on, son, fuck me hard!"

I was still getting my sea legs when it came to being on top. I teased him, letting my big cockhead rub against his asshole. I ran my hands up and down his legs, massaging the spot where the thigh became a round hairy butt.

"We don't have all night."

My teasing was having an effect. But now I was in command. He didn't get to order me around.

"Why don't you beg for it."

He resisted, then I saw him switch to the role of a passive, obedient slave.

"Please, son, fuck me."

"That's more like it." I entered him quickly, rounding the corner and mashing my hips into his fat butt. Maximus shrieked in pain. I *had* grown bigger, hadn't I?

His hands clawed at the straw mattress, and he wriggled to get me out, but I just held there until he relaxed. Yellow dust came out of his ass.

"Did I hurt you?"

"No, son."

"It's 'Sir' to you now." I glared at him sternly.

"No, sir. You didn't hurt me, sir."

I put my hands on Maximus's feet for a good grip and pumped him hard. He pounded the mattress, clenched his teeth, and moaned.

"Keep going, sir," I loved his enthusiasm.

My ass was still throbbing from its recent encounter with the soldier's rock-hard dick, so it didn't take long to reach climax.

"You want my seed inside you?"

Maximus nodded swiftly.

"Good. Here it comes." With a burst of energy, I

pounded his back wall instead of turning the corner. The resistance made me come right away.

"Oh, shit, Maximus. You've got a fuckable ass."

"Yes, sir." I leaned down and kissed him while the final spurts of my cum drained into the beast of a man. Yellow dust escaped when I withdrew.

Applause filled the room. The whole garrison had returned and witnessed my performance. I slipped on my tunic and snuck away while the soldiers all asked if they could have a go with Maximus.

Outside, I nearly tripped over Longinus.

"You scared me! How did you find me?"

He frowned. "I followed the dust clouds, you whore."

His words stung. "I did it to keep us safe!"

Longinus sighed. "I saw you. How did fucking that guard keep us safe?"

I shook my head. "You weren't there at the portal. You don't know what you're talking about."

He pointed at my cock. "Look how big you got. I don't know if I can take it now."

I looked down. I was much bigger. I was soft, and it peeked out from under my tunic. I needed a loincloth for the first time in my life.

Longinus mused, "We must be safe if we have time to fight."

"We are safe!" I told him about the new emperor.

"Let's find an inn." Longinus looked weary. "I'm famished and tired."

CATCH AND RELEASE

We got a room with a large bed and a distant view of the bay. Downstairs, we ate sausage and barley bread with cheese and wine.

Seating was scarce. A great hulk of a man asked if he could join us. He was clever and talkative. I noticed him touch Longinus's arm each time he made a point. Longinus pretended not to notice. The man bought us absinthium. I disliked the drink, and its effects were dizzying.

Longinus and the mysterious stranger were getting more physical. Touching became rubbing. I had no right to complain, but it was purposeless. I fucked to finish my flirting. My flirting was a tool for gathering intelligence. This was just two big men getting chummy.

I refused a second serving of absinthium. By the time Longinus reached the bottom of the cup, he and his new friend were embracing. I politely excused myself and went to bed.

In the middle of the night, I was awoken by knocking. Did Longinus lose his key? Was he bringing that oaf up here to fuck?

I opened the door and saw the innkeeper's daughter.

"I'm terribly sorry, sir," she said, "but your friend was kidnapped."

My heart fell. "Was it that big guy?"

She nodded. "He works at the Ludus: the gladiator school. He gets strong men drunk and then knocks them out. I can't believe my father didn't intervene."

I had seen her father. He made me look like an athlete.

She handed me a purse. It was the satchel that belonged to Longinus.

"He threw this under the bar. I know he meant it for you."

I nodded. I handed her a Denarius.

"Oh, no, sir, I couldn't accept–"

"A good friend of mine taught me never to refuse money. I am passing the lesson to you."

I got directions to the school. It was in a dirty part of town. Sick kittens ran from starving dogs covered in mange. Garbage rotted on the cobblestones.

The Ludus Capuensis was a massive complex. It was quiet. I walked right in. Then two giant dogs on chains barked and snarled. I was soaked in their spittle. A guard came running.

"What do you want?"

I thought about my strategy on the way over. This might work.

"I came to see...oh what was his name?"

"Everyone is asleep."

"But he only just left the inn." I folded my arms.

The guard said, "Oh, tall guy?"

I nodded.

"That's Gaetanus."

I dropped an invisible plumb line, Roman sign language for "Exactly."

I said, "He was interested in, uh, my services."

"He was drunk. He may need a rain check."

My jealousy compelled me to ask an imprudent

question. "I thought he bumfucked that big muscle guy."

The guard straightened up. "He may be tall, but he's too small to do that." This guard knew Gaetanus well.

I kept bluffing. "That explains why he requested my services." I lifted the tunic a tiny bit to fully expose the head of my cock.

The guard licked his lips. "It's late. What do you need?"

"I mean, it's funny because that fellow he brought in is triple my size. Maybe it's too much of a good thing."

The guard was intrigued. "Wait, show me your cock again."

I shrugged. "No charge." I lifted my tunic entirely, exposing my very big dick.

The guard shook his head like a fly was in his ear. "You're telling me the new recruit is three times your size? Impossible!"

I laughed. "That's what I thought until I pissed next to him. You wouldn't believe it."

"I think you're lying." He folded his arms.

"One Denarius says he has the biggest dick you have ever seen."

I produced a Denarius from a pocket. I didn't dare show the satchel.

"He's passed out drunk."

"Even soft, he's a giant. We can just lift his tunic. He'll never know."

The guard nodded. He grabbed a ring of keys and walked me to cages where men were kept captive like animals.

I tested him. "Do we have to open the cage? What if he got out?"

The guard shook his head.

"He still has a collar."

My strategy struck a wall. But I had to go on.

"He could grab the keys from you."

He pointed to a leather strap around his neck. "I keep the collar keys separate."

I persisted. "Let me see."

He took the necklace of keys and handed it to me. It was perfect timing. We arrived at the cage that held Longinus.

He unlocked it, and we stepped in.

I knelt by his head. "What happened? He's bleeding!"

"Gaetanus must have roughed him up a little." The guard licked his lips, eager to see what lay under Longinus's tunic.

I did three things at once. First, I pinched Longinus on the ear as hard as possible to revive him. Next, I pulled back his tunic to reveal the beautiful curse between his legs. At the same time, I unlocked his collar when the guard stood still and touched himself, completely distracted.

"Oh, sorry, here." I handed him the necklace. He took it absently. "Pretty big?"

"I've seen bigger," he lied. He wanted to keep his money.

"Where is your honor? Where did you see bigger?"

"Umm, nowhere." He was drooling.

"Touch it; he doesn't care."

The guard went to his knees and raised Longinus's heavy meat to his mouth. He tried to put it in, but it wouldn't fit. He stared, silently mouthing an incantation or holding an imaginary conversation.

I looked Longinus in the face. He was awake and assessing the situation. I pantomimed his neck collar opening. He gave a subtle nod. In silence, he removed it. I chatted with the cock-crazed guard to mask any noise.

"I'll give you the Denarius, even though I won."

The guard paid me no attention.

I could probably say anything, so I did. "Consider it

payment for when you pass out because he's going to put you to sleep with his legs."

"Wait, What?" That was the last thing I heard him say.

Longinus locked the guard in a knee chokehold. He struggled, turned red, then passed out. Longinus held him a few more seconds, then checked to be sure he was breathing. The last thing we needed was another murder. We didn't have much time.

"Here." He tossed me a bunch of keys. "Go let everyone free."

"Why?"

Longinus explained while we ran from cage to cage, letting slaves go. "If you were looking for a fugitive, what would make it harder?"

"A lot more fugitives."

He made the plumb line to signal I was correct.

❧ 28 ❧

GOOD CHRISTIANS

Under cover of night, a dozen slaves scattered to the four winds. We made a beeline back to the inn, gathered our few measly possessions, and hit the Via Atellana, which formed a straight line from Capua to Neapolis. But it passed right through the center of town first. The town square was a hollow star. It was the meeting of the Via Appia, the Via Atellana, the Via Traiana, and the Via Popilia. Coming from one of these grand roads, we heard shouts. I heard the familiar sound of two dogs barking and feared the worst.

Longinus was going door to door, examining the lintels. That's right! We needed to find a carved cross. I ran in the opposite direction around the square.

"Here!" Longinus called out and pounded on the heavy wooden door of a plain building. Above the door was a cross carved almost as though it were a crack in the wood. After Nero blamed them for the fire, Christians had to hide in plain sight.

The dogs drew closer. Longinus pounded again, and the door flew open. A sparkly-eyed Greek man with a full beard said, "Peace, brother, for he is risen."

I knew there was a correct response, but Pius never told us.

I grabbed the man by his arm and formed the unique V-shape with my fingers. He kissed me on the lips.

"Brethren, come join us." He pulled us in and softly but swiftly closed the door behind us. Moments later, the horrible barking of the dogs reverberated off the facades facing the town center. I sighed in relief when they stopped growing louder and began to fade.

The Greek was named Stephanos, and he looked good in a tunic. He ushered us out of the foyer into a simple living space with a kitchen. "What brings you gentlemen to the Capua Cult of the Risen Christ?"

Longinus gave a summary of our predicament. The handsome Greek bent to retrieve a pot from the lower shelf; a perfect ass stretched his tunic. When he stood, the ass ate the fabric. Both of us stared in awe.

Stephanos giggled. "This? I can tell you like it." He removed his tunic, revealing powerful legs topped with two ham-sized buttocks. He wiggled, and they bounced rhythmically up and down, occasionally smacking into each other.

I was rock hard, and so was Longinus. Stephanos nodded his head knowingly. I see you need sex magic. He pointed at me. "You, definitely, I shall have you."

He pointed to Longinus. "There's a chance for you, but it is as slim as you are thick."

He wasted no time. He needed sex magic as much as we did. How beautiful that something so mutually pleasurable could be a source for mutual gain.

I looked at the huge, perfect butt with dimpled sides and a pretty pink hole buried at the bottom. I spread his cheeks far apart and used my tongue to loosen his hole. He inhaled hard through his teeth. I was doing it right.

With my mouth engaged, I had to wave Longinus over to us. He may still have been angry at me or ashamed of his reckless acts. My next move, stroking his cock, was a silent truce. I held the end and guided it to my hole.

I reached for Stephanos's cock with my other hand, but it wasn't there. He was like me! Like I had once been. I found a tiny pair of balls and a nipple-sized penis drooling pre-cum. Just as I would have once done, he moved my hand away and pushed that incredible butt harder into my face.

It was no surprise I would be the spoiled one, taking Longinus in the rear and having Stephanos in front of me, hungry for my ever-growing cock. The magic was going to be powerful.

The big-assed Greek asked, "So what does your magic do?"

I pulled my mouth off his winking flesh tunnel and said, "Mine makes my dick bigger."

"And you, Longinus?"

"Wealth. Gold."

"Oh, that's a fun one!" Before I could ask about his magic, the Greek pulled my head into his bottom again. I licked and spit until he was slippery.

My ass was still sloppy with Magnus's spunk, so I didn't need any help.

I stood, and as Longinus pushed into me, I drove into Stephanos. The room grew white with steamy smoke. Stephanos's long-strangled sigh was the exact sound I would make when Longinus penetrated me, so we formed a small chorus in unison. I felt the back of our host's rectum and pushed my way further. He squealed like a pig. As Longinus made his way into me, I stretched wider and wider and felt my dick grow bigger and bigger. We found our rhythm quickly, and soon I was dazed, staring at the massive cheeks of Stephanos as they rippled and danced from my heavy pounding. Stephanos was in ecstasy. His soft moans and ragged breaths were interrupted by an occasional loud cry of "That's it!"

Longinus would never be easy to take, but he was worth the hard work. He caused a trembling in my bowel that felt like scratching a mosquito bite. My legs were in use, grinding ever deeper into the Greek. But Longinus took them out from under me with his masterful deep fucking. Then my breaths were ragged, too.

Stephanos held my wrist and put it below his crotch. He was drooling clear pre-come like a leaky pot. I tasted it, then coughed white dust everywhere. The magic was growing.

Longinus picked up speed, slamming me harder into the sexy Greek with the best ass in Rome. "Oh, Oh!" Longinus was moving towards a precipice. He fucked furiously until I thought I might burst. "Shit!" He cried aloud and unleashed a warm flow of semen into my ass. The intense sensation created an orgasm in my ass that caused me to spasm and shake before releasing my sperm into Stephanos. I still held one hand under his tiny penis. I used the other to rub his chest and tiny nipples. I knew from my own experience that size had no effect on output. Stephanos, hands on his thick thighs, sprayed my hand with thick white cum. I fed it to him; he lapped it up like a thirsty farm animal.

My cock didn't soften. Longinus was also stiff. When I withdrew from Stephanos, his anus formed a large open ring.

"The store is still open," the twinkly-eyed Greek offered. Longinus stepped in, pressing into the firm round buttocks. I moved around and planted my feet behind Longinus. It had been a few days, and I had grown a lot. To ease the entry, I farted cum into my palm, rubbing it in his tight hole and along the length of my shaft. Synchronized as we were, I forced my way into Longinus as he fought his way into the Greek bottom. The two men cried out like women. I felt oddly guilty. I understood the guilt Longinus must have felt his whole life. He trembled, pressing his palm against my hips to keep me from pushing deeper.

Stephanos nodded his head, and Longinus pressed in further. I waited for a signal, but none came. I had grown too big. I reversed to withdraw, but Longinus grabbed my buttock and pressed me back in. He rocked his hips, forcing me deeper.

"Aah, shit! Fuck! Ow!" His pain broke my heart. But he wouldn't let me out.

Stephanos sobbed. "You're so fucking huge!" With his powerful legs, he thrust backward, impaling himself. The thrust knocked Longinus off balance, and he fell into me. My cock rounded the corner and wedged deep inside Longinus. My hips pressed into his buttocks. I felt Stephanos's giant buttocks press against my fingers where I held Longinus. We were joined as one.

We fucked gently at first, building to a furious pace as lust and desire won out over fear and pain. The last remnants of cum from Magnus and Longinus leaked out of my sloppy hole and down one leg. At the front of our chain, Stephanos produced so much pre-cum that it overflowed in Longinus's cupped palm and fell to the floor in loud drops.

I ran my fingers up and down Longinus's sides, rippling with muscle. He was shivering from pain. In that instant, I understood his struggle. To want to be buried deep in your beloved, knowing how much it would hurt them...it was torture. I wanted him to know how good he felt to me. I called on my memories with him, the intense pleasure he gave me, and used them to create strokes and rhythm to match his. My thrusts could never be so powerful, so skilled, but I tried to imitate him. It worked. Longinus became warm to the touch, and his sweat ran not from pain but from exertion.

"Oh, Formosus, is this what you feel?"

"Describe it."

Between pants, Longinus said, "I...feel...like...my whole body...is coming."

"That's it."

The best part was that the more pleasure I gave him, the more intense my own phallic sensations grew. The building orgasm was like a long sneeze that never entirely comes. I shivered, sending the vibration down the chain. Longinus shivered, and Stephanos let out a moan of intense satisfaction. After many months of hosting Longinus in my anal cavity, I knew what the Greek man felt.

We continued for much of the watch, passing pleasure up and down the chain from one body to another until it was impossible to continue. Stephanos had a loud, feminine orgasm.

"Oh yes, yes, oh sweet Jesus Christ, ohhhhhh, unnnnnh!"

I felt Longinus contract around my cock as he emptied himself into the massive butt of the writhing Greek, whose tiny penis had left a large puddle beneath him. The contractions milked my huge cock, forcing my semen to release in a sudden explosion. Longinus gasped. He reached behind and pressed me deeper, so my cum got lost deep in his belly. Exhausted, the three of us clung to one another for support. When we broke, cum came dribbling out of Stephanos and Longinus. I caught some with my tongue and shared it in a three-man kiss.

Although neither Longinus nor I had slept for long, the energy and magic had revived us. We were wide awake.

"Longinus asked, "What about you, Stephanos? What is your magic?"

"As crows, your magic chooses you. It is usually very personal to you, reflecting deep, lifelong material desires. Longinus, you must feel an unconscious need to be wealthy. Money is not evil, but the love of money is.

If you have enough, you can focus on more important matters in the spiritual world. And Formosus, it's safe to say that you were once the way I am now. You wanted more choices and a stronger male role in sex."

"I don't understand. What magic chose you?"

"The very opposite of yours, Formosus. I was huge, almost like Longinus, and my ass was flat, not nearly as nice as yours or his. Because of my size and my ugly rump, I was always put in the active role with every man and boy I met. They would beg me to fuck them, then scream for me to stop. I wanted desperately to stop causing pain for others. And I only wanted to play the passive role. So, my ass swelled, and my huge cock shrank and shrank until it became what you see now."

"Oh, I get it."

Longinus nodded, too. "I think I may have ended up like you, Stephanos, had I not met Formosus. He makes me proud to be the way I am."

Stephanos nodded. "Unlike you, I never wished to be the man. No one would dream of doing to me what I so desperately wanted. But now..."

I jumped in. "You have the best ass in Capua if not all of Rome. You must receive constant advances."

He winked. "I take all comers. And there are many, many comers."

I was still curious, "You said that as crows, our magic chooses us. What happens when we are nymphos, or Lion?"

"The magic frees itself and allows you to choose its purpose."

"So, what did your magic do for you tonight?"

He smiled. "Once you can wish for anything, it grows wearisome to always wish for yourself. I wished that you and Longinus would ascend to nymphos, be joined as Adelphopoii, and live a long, prosperous life by the sea."

The nymphos was the second rank in the Mithraic

hierarchy, but I had no idea what he meant by Adelphopoii.

Stephanos explained, "Sometimes, two men are so close, it must be recognized before God. Adelphopoiesis is the means to join two men as a family. It makes you brothers under Christ and even under the laws of Rome."

"Who can perform such a ritual?"

"I can. First, you must ascend a level. You will not lose your magic, but it may begin to change. Are you ready now?"

Longinus and I stared into each other's eyes. It was time to dive deeper into the mysteries of Mithraism, and we longed for the bond. We knew this without saying a single word. We nodded in unison.

"Follow me!"

❊ 29 ❊

A WEDDING

In the larder, there was a false shelf on hinges. It led to a spiral stone staircase. Deep under the house, we arrived at a Mithraeum. Here were the brothers of the congregation, at work preparing a feast. I recognized several soldiers from our entry at the gates of Capua. Maximus was under a table, repairing a leg. He saw me and then Longinus. His eyes lit up.

"Salve, Formosus. You don't know how glad we are you found us."

"I thought you were chasing us."

"The Ludus has its own dogs and guards to track so-called escapees. By law, it's not escape if you were put there against your will!"

He sized up Longinus, feeling his arms and back. "I can see why they wanted him."

"If you knew, why didn't you help?" I asked.

"We did. Do you not have magic now? With magic, all things are possible, even the impossible. Only a few gladiators have ever escaped the Ludus."

Stephanos joined us and, wrapping his arms around Maximus, planted a kiss on his lips.

"I see you've met Stephanos. He's my brother. We are joined. Is he not the best piece of ass you ever fucked?"

Stephanos smiled at us. "You got competition, Max." he indicated Longinus with his head.

Maximus felt under Longinus's tunic like a physician examining a patient. He pulled his hand away as if burnt by fire.

"Zeus! That's a big one. Yes, you have me beat."

Stephanos pointed to me, "He's growing with magic, so you may have another rival."

"I sampled him. The clouds of red smoke were powerful magic indeed."

I stepped forward. "You saw them?"

"Yes. Of course. I can't say anything if you haven't given me the handshake."

The feast was very strict on ceremony. The local Pater, a wind-worn soldier, read incantations, which we recited back. Food came between chapters. The wine was warm and tasted of bitter mushroom. As the ceremony continued, I saw shapes made only of shadow and light hovering in the room. As I followed one with my eyes, I overheard Stephanos say, "Formosus sees the archangels now."

A few minutes later, Longinus saw them too. The ritual began.

We were given some noises to make, like crackling and popping, 'aya eye yee,' 'mmm,' sharp intakes of breath, and dozens more. This would allow the protection of the archangels to carry us to the one true God. It all grew hazy as the mushroom wine won out over everything, and I was soon in a very real dream, floating through layers of stone and dirt until I burst into the sunlight, rising rapidly to the clouds. I turned my head to see Longinus beside me. His smile in the face of such fearful heights made me relax. He was so much braver than me. The angels swooped and dove around us, testing us to see if we would jump. When I put my hand in Longinus's, they stopped. They could see nothing would scare us now.

We fell into darkness and landed like a feather on the table in the Mithraeum. The Pater instructed us to disrobe so that we may be part of the feast. Soldiers, bakers, and slaves stood shoulder to shoulder around us, caressing us and arousing our cocks. Mouths, hands, and anuses were everywhere, sucking, rubbing, stroking, mounting, consuming our sexual bodies like cheese and barley bread. Instead of smoke, Longinus gave off gold coins. My cock swelled and stretched far larger than I had imagined possible. With a loud clatter, Longinus shot hundreds of gold coins from the tip of his penis. The tip of my penis fell suddenly, smacking into my knee. The magic stopped. It was no longer our unconscious desires being fulfilled. I wished for all the Christian Mithraism of Capua to be safe from persecution. Purple and grey dust swirled around the congregation, blessing and protecting them.

The magic we raised was powerful. Stephanos gave Longinus a grain sack to carry all the gold that had multiplied while we were stupefied and sexually serviced by the congregation. My cock had reached uncomfortable dimensions. My size was less than Longinus's, but I was still huge. It was a turning point - our magic could no longer serve us. Any more gold and there would be too much to carry. If I got any bigger, I would never be able to do anything. Then I noticed my thin arms had grown into thick, tawny limbs with large biceps and triceps. I looked at my legs, and they were quite thick as well. My shoulders were heavy on my frame, and my back supported them with solid muscles. I was no longer puerile - I was virile. Standing next to Longinus, we made a real pair.

The Adelphopoiesis was the last ceremony.

Stephanos recited lines from some loose-leaf papers containing tales about Jesus Christ. He said, "Owe no one anything except to love each other, for the one who loves another has fulfilled the law. For you were called to freedom, brothers. Do not use your freedom as an opportunity for the flesh, but through love, serve one another. Having purified your souls by your obedience to the truth for a sincere brotherly love, love one another earnestly from a pure heart."

We clasped hands, my hand no longer small and helpless in Longinus's grip. I was as much his protector now as he mine. I had broken him from prison and could help shoulder the heavy bag of gold. We kissed deeply to seal our bond and were made brothers in Christ. We were no longer crows; we were bridegrooms under Mithras. As we kissed, a cloud of smoke escaped and blew up the stairwell. Our magic told us we were ready to leave.

30
NEW CITY, NEW FRIENDS

Neapolis was a Greek city. The language was a mixture of Latin and Greek.

Capua had whored herself out to Rome, and in exchange, its citizens enjoyed peace and protection courtesy of soldiers like Maximus.

Neapolis had a different energy. They had signed with Rome, but they did not ask for Rome's protection. The magistrate had a considerable force of thugs and vigiles who kept a chaotic harmony in a delicate balance with the forces of darkness. It was never formally stated, but escaped slaves knew they had nothing to fear in Neapolis. Slavery existed in Roman households within the city, but sales were forbidden. Greek households found the practice repugnant. Capua had walls; Neapolis had harbors. They traded with the great Islands like Crete, Rhodes and Sicilia. Carthage and the rest of Northern Africa traded so heavily with Neapolis that it was common to see Africans living alongside Romans and Greeks.

The city smelled like garlic, liquamen, rotten fruit, and roses.

The ten-mile journey had left us famished and thirsty. We found a vendor cooking flatbread with cheese and herbs in a hot oven. He gave us each a pomegranate juice. It cost only two quadrans. We strolled along the waterfront, watching the fishermen straighten their nets. Smoked octopus on a stick helped round out the flavors of the flatbread. Above us were the hills where we hoped to make our home. We climbed the zigzagging streets until we reached the top of the highest hill. This was too high. When we grew old, we would struggle to reach these heights. If we wanted smoked octopus, it would be an hour's hike. Upon descending, we rounded the hill and discovered a busy street called Decumanus Superiore. There were inns and market stalls selling everything from apples to wool.

This would be home. A few blocks up one of the alleyways, or *cardini*, there were lots for sale. The Taberna Superiore was a welcome sight. We bought a room for a week. The bed was large and comfortable. We were wed as brothers now, and this could have been our first time fucking as a married couple, but we were tired and content to fall asleep in each other's arms as the sun set over Baia and Pozzuoli.

The owner of the Inn introduced us to a widow who needed to sell a plot of land two blocks up the hill. It was high enough to give a panoramic view of the bay and the sea beyond Pozzuoli. She asked fifteen Aurea for the plot, which was adjacent to the aqueduct. The city charged us one Aurea and twelve Denarii for access to the fresh water. There was a brickworks on the Decumanus Superiore. We saved on costs by hauling bricks ourselves. With my virile frame, I could carry the same load as Longinus.

The Taberna was an ideal temporary home while we built our dream house. The house's design included a terrace and an altana on the roof. It was summer. We were grateful for the aqueduct keeping us from heatstroke. We wet our kerchiefs and wore them around our necks. Stripped to our loincloths, we attracted the attention of the neighbors.

It was August; the Neapolitan sun was merciless. We made it a priority to get the roof built so we had a place to escape the mid-August sun. Many of the men in the neighborhood stripped to their loincloths like us. Gastron, a chubby young man who lived alone in his family's home, was fond of stopping by to lend a hand. He called Longinus *Demippos*, and I was *Andrippos*, but we had no idea what the names meant. He always volunteered to do work requiring much bending, like setting tile or painting the kickboards. He was pleasant. His Latin was overrun with Greek, but we followed much of his words. He was twenty. He had gone fishing with his father and two little brothers when a storm came and destroyed the boat. Heavy Gastron was a floater, but not the others. They were never found. His mother was overcome with grief and took her life. She left him enough money to survive until he could learn a trade. We were teaching him masonry and home design, which was what he wanted to do. It was a great arrangement.

At the Inn, the owner nearly fell out of his chair when we told him the nicknames that Gastron had given us. Demippos meant 'half-horse,' and Andrippos was 'man-horse.'

The next day, I caught Gastron stealing glances at our bulging loincloths. I wasn't sure how to bridge the subject, so I pulled a stunt. I got blue paint on my loincloth.

"Oh no!" I shouted. "I'll be right back." I stripped off the loincloth in front of Gastron, and he nearly fainted when my enormous cock tumbled out and bounced between my kneecaps.

I turned to Longinus. "Demippos, yours is filthy. Hand it here." Longinus pulled it off. I worried the tubby young man might suffer a paroxysm. Then I turned to him.

"Gastron, may I wash your loincloth? It's August, and we all know how sweaty they get."

He nodded and removed his, revealing a furry round bottom and small balls with a very short, thin, rock-hard cock. It was not as small as mine had been, but it definitely couldn't penetrate a vagina, let alone an anus. He was blushing with shame.

I stepped close to take the loincloth, and my equine phallus rubbed against his little pecker. It was a demonstration of the superiority of my giant cock. Wordlessly, he kneeled. He put the head in his mouth with the skill one would expect from a big eater. He surprised me by going down past the tonsils. I was astonished when he took the entire length, the head dangling halfway to his stomach inside his throat.

Longinus drew close, and Gastron lifted his fat furry ass in the air, wiggling it to lure him in. My brother-husband slapped Gastron with his cock. The chubby man coughed on my cock, took the phlegm and spit, then rubbed it in and around his anus. He took a second glob and rubbed it on Longinus's pole. Gastron was stuffed at both ends. He grabbed greedily at my balls as if they were apples. He wanted to feel big cocks and balls in every way possible. Behind him, he was holding Longinus by the testicles. Longinus was only a third of the way in. He dared not go deeper on this man unless he knew he could handle it. I sighed, realizing my magical growth had given me the same restrictions.

Gastron leaned forward until Longinus popped out, then hauled my cock out of his mouth. He rotated and began sucking on Longinus. I saw his well-stretched hole and thought perhaps I could give it a go. Instead of stopping at the wall, I pushed past and plowed deep inside the furry bottom. With his mouth full of cock, his cries of protest sounded like pig grunts. They didn't last. As I fucked him gently, they turned to moans of contentment. I let my thrusts get ever more forceful until I heard a squealing protest, then I backed away a notch or two. I kept it right there, up to my balls, pounding hard but not furiously. Between the sucking and the contented moans, Gastron resembled a lamb or piglet getting milk.

A green magic came out of the pig boy's ass, and aqua blue went out of his mouth. The green meant growth, so I wished Gastron could grow larger genitals. I had everything I wanted. I was sure that Gastron was a far more talented cocksucker than me. He put things in his mouth constantly, so it made sense. He wasn't as gifted at taking it up the bum, but it wasn't fair to compare someone like me who had been doing it for so long.

Longinus threw his head back, stroking Gastron's ears. "Oh shit, kid, you're fucking amazing." He doubled over and shot his load deep into the chubby boy's throat. Aqua-blue smoke filled our half-finished house.

Gastron took great gasps and sucked air through his teeth. He reached back and softly rubbed my nipples with his chubby hand. It was the right move.

I pounded his hole without mercy. He whined and cried, but the words he called were "yes" and "fuck me, Andrippos!"

I watched my new powerful cock stretch apart the furry butt cheeks. The power was intoxicating. I was forcing my huge fat cock into this young man's ass, and he was begging for it. Then his little penis sprayed cum on the floor. It was too much, and I let go without warning.

"Oh, fuck here I come!" A deluge of sperm filled Gastron's fat, furry butt. He had tears in his eyes and a delighted smile on his face. A giant cloud of green smoke leaked from his ass like a fart. It wrapped itself around his genitals; when it cleared, he was thicker and much longer, nearly average.

"What did you do?" He felt his new, fuller-sized genitals still dripping with sperm.

"Getting fucked by a huge dick makes you bigger." It was a fib, but it was more believable than the truth.

"I'm coming back for more." There were tears of joy clouding his vision. I can have children now.

After Gastron limped home, I asked Longinus what his magic would do.

"I wished that Gastron would have a family again."

For days, these double-ended horse cock penetrations became a thrice daily break from the bricklaying and cement smoothing. Gastron grew a little more each time, and the hard labor made his belly shrink.

In less than a month, the bricks we laid became our home. It was just in need of carpentry. By now, Gastron had a massive swinging tool. He held his head high at the market, where he flirted with all the ladies. I was certain he would soon choose one to be his bride and fill her womb with babies.

31

SILVANUS

One morning in late August, the mountain on the other side of the bay blew plumes of steam into the air. The locals call it Vesuvius. It was followed by a small earthquake, which knocked a few bricks out of place, but otherwise, it was harmless. Still, we saw hundreds of ships set out across the bay to land in the ports of Neapolis and Misenum. They wanted to be as far away from Vesuvius as possible. Gastron climbed to our home and asked if we were going to help.

"How can we help?" I asked.

"We'll meet the boats as they land and offer to share our living quarters."

It was true our house was almost habitable, but we remained at the inn for the food and other conveniences. Selfishly, I thought it would be good to find a strong lad with carpentry skills from among the exiles, so we could put him to work finishing the place. We were at a point where neither of us knew how to complete the job. It wasn't true charity but it seemed like an opportunity worth exploring.

We worked our way down to the waterfront, crossing the Decumanus Maggiore and the Decumanus Inferiore before arriving at the busy harbor. A beautiful young woman wearing a yellow linen toga approached us.

"Hello, I'm Livia. Until the volcano is quiet, I am looking for a temporary shelter. Can you help me?"

Gastron wasted no time; he took her by the hand and left us, escorting her up the hill to his home. He had room for dozens more but clearly didn't want a crowd.

Just as we had hoped, we saw a man with a hammer, a saw, and other tools of the carpentry trade. He asked, "Are you gentlemen in need of a woodworker? I have a big hammer and a sharp saw." He stood in such a way as to let us see the ripples of muscle under his tunic. He had a well-proportioned cock that swayed in and out of sight under his tunic.

He saw me staring. "I was in such a rush; I forgot my loincloth!"

Longinus spoke, "We require a carpenter, and you look suitable. Do you have a place to stay?"

"I do not." He bent to tie a loose strap on his sandal, revealing more of his well-built frame and his low-hanging testicles.

I asked, "What's your name?"

"Silvanus." He did not reach for our arm. He was not in the cult of Mithras. "I'm Silvanus of Herculaneum."

"Where is your family?"

"I have none. I'm a freedman."

Longinus spoke. "We are nearing completion of our house and require a carpenter to finish the trim, build shutters, and other light tasks. In exchange, we will pay for your room at the nearby inn."

"If it's all the same, I will gladly sleep in the house until it is finished." Silvanus was perfect.

"In that case, we will give you the coins we would have spent housing you."

Silvanus smiled brightly. His handsome features

looked spectacular, framed by a lovely grin. We walked up the hill to our home and showed him around.

He nodded, making mental calculations, then said, "This is a three-week job if I work full days.

"If I do this regularly, you will have no problems."

"That is ideal. Three sestertii per day, will that do?"

Silvanus nodded. "Plus the cost of materials."

"Yes, of course."

The sun beat down intensely. It was high noon.

To seal our agreement, we shared wine from the amphora.

Silvanus drank quickly.

"I was so thirsty!" He cried, taking another.

Longinus and I took him to the edge of the property and showed him the aqueduct.

He stripped off his tunic and rubbed a wet rag over his sweaty body. Unclothed, he was a Greek statue come to life, except his genitals were considerably larger than those of the modest youths preserved in marble.

"Men, I'll make your house beautiful. It is already a great building, but with me, you will see it reach perfection." We returned to the house. Silvanus was content to stay naked, basking in our admiration. He poured another cup from the amphora.

Longinus was both practical and seductive. "We should show you the bed."

We escorted him to the upper floor, where the bed looked out on the bay.

Silvanus was making short work of the wine. Then he stunned us. He made a drunken proposition. "I'll get in bed with you, but there's no way you guys are gonna fuck my ass. I'm pretty big, yet next to you guys, I'm nothing."

"How do you know?"

"I'm a carpenter; I have an eye for measuring." He smiled and winked.

Together, we helped our drunk companion down the hill. He stripped off his tunic and lay bare naked, face down on the bed.

Longinus and I climbed into the large bed, surrounding our new carpenter friend. He reached into our loincloths and let out a startled cry.

"There is just no fucking way!"

I put my arms around his neck. "You're a very big man. I love a good fuck."

Silvanus pulled my head down and kissed my mouth. His long tongue swept my tonsils, making my cock grow hard.

He stood on the bed and put his long, thick meat in my mouth. Longinus curled up beside me and sucked on mine. It wasn't fair; Longinus had no one to suck him. But Silvanus twisted around until we formed a triangle, each man sucking another. I had it easy. Silvanus was well-hung, yet he fit perfectly down my throat. Neither Longinus nor Silvanus could work their lips around the two giant cocks in the room.

I thought about the time I spent at the inn with Longinus and how he always wanted to be the one putting it in the other. I loved the full sensation he gave me, but there was always pain and agony before things began feeling good. Judging by the size and shape of the cock in my mouth, I knew Silvanus would feel good immediately.

I took his huge tool out of my mouth and licked the tip. It was so perfect! Silvanus was built for fucking.

I bent over, exposing my ass. Silvanus yanked his mouth from Longinus and put his tongue against my shitter. I felt his warm saliva coat the walls. Bent over as I was, I put Longinus in my mouth.

I saw stars when Silvanus rammed inside me. He wasn't as big, but he was shaped differently. My ass wasn't used to him, so it clenched and caused me to let out a stifled scream.

"Did I hurt you?"

I shook my head. It was already starting to feel good. He was big enough to push past my back wall and knew how to do it. His fucking was artful; he ground his hips into me with force, precision, and speed.

"You feel so good," the Greek said.

He was talking about how good my ass was, but I answered, "Oh yes, I do feel good."

I let Longinus fuck my throat until it became clear he wanted more. I motioned with my eyes.

I pushed Silvanus onto his back, then leaned forward so my ass was exposed in the air. I felt Longinus press against me. I nodded. He pressed forward until his cock Head was wedged in my ass next to Silvanus's shaft. My hole felt like it would burst.

As Longinus pressed further, Silvanus said, "Shit! You're so fucking huge!" He cupped Longinus's balls and kissed his lips, then put his tongue in his mouth.

I pounded the bed with my fists, regretting saying yes to Longinus until I finally felt him slip past Silvanus.

The Greek was stunned. "You aren't even three-fourths in, and you are way deeper than me!"

The two men sawed their way in and out of my ass, rubbing against each other. There was so much pressure where the two men were thickest; I looked like an amphora as my huge jutting cock poured clear fluid onto the floor behind Silvanus's Head. There was no magic this time. The newness of Silvanus and his lack of initiation into the cult of Mithras and the Risen Christ were enough to suppress the magic.

Silvanus kissed Longinus again, holding his ass and slapping it. Soon, the double fucking became two dicks grinding and rubbing together in my convenient hole. They were bringing each other to orgasm. Jealousy aside, it felt great to be the ribbon that bound the two men together. It felt even better when I shot a big load in the air. It landed on Silvanus's face.

"Oh fuck, I'm coming, Longinus said. And in that same familiar spot somewhere in my belly, he coated me with his semen.

Silvanus's eyes opened wider. "Is that your cum?" Longinus nodded.

He took a big blob of my come from his face and fingered his asshole.

His face looked like someone battling constipation. "Oh Formosus, oh fuck, you feel so good with your man's come inside you, all over my dick. Oh shit. Oh!" He squeezed his eyes shut and made a trumpet noise with his nose. "This is it!"

Further down, closer to the asshole, but still very deep, I felt Silvanus come. It was hotter than Longinus's. I saw his dangling balls draw up tight and pulsate over and over. His cum was too much for my highly pressurized rectum, and some sprayed out, coating his and Longinus's balls with the thick white syrup. We tried to pull out, but Longinus held his cock hostage. The two slid together, giving bittersweet relief to my stretched anus. With them came the deluge of mixed semen. Longinus cupped his hand and fed it to me. Silvanus lapped some up like a second dog at the water bowl, then stuck his finger in my ass to make more come out. When my hole was sufficiently drained, we separated.

Longinus smiled at Silvanus. "I hope you saved some come for me. I'm next. You and Formosus are going to fuck me together."

As wonderful as that sounded, it wouldn't happen that day.

Our house shook when a boom louder than anything I had ever heard reverberated across the water. The volcano had exploded. We rushed to our balcony to see a cloud so tall and thick that it appeared to reach the sun. We watched the cloud blow gently to the south, away from Neapolis. We wandered down to the inn, asking people if they knew what had happened. The consensus was that the eruption had no hot lava. This sounded good until we saw a transparent, shimmering cloud of heat roll down the mountain on the southern and western slopes. Herculaneum was at the base of the western slope. Silvanus cringed in horror as the cloud set fire to his city, immediately turning the sea into a boiling cauldron. The boiling sea water put out the fire but smothered the town in thick black mud.

I held Silvanus as he wept for his friends who stayed behind. The ash plume came down from the moon and buried Pompeii. We rushed up to our house when ash began descending on us. Silvanus grabbed a palm frond to push the ash off the roof. We brought him water and fruit to keep him going. The cloud fell until the second watch. We saw the moon again.

In case of any clouds of heat, we decided all three to sleep at the Inn. The Taberna was filled with the chatter of dozens of Neapolitans wondering what would happen next. I fell into a dreamless sleep, cradled by Longinus and Silvanus.

EPILOGUE

It is now one year since the eruption. Life in Neapolis returned to normal almost immediately. It is the character of this city to simply march over rubble piles and get on with one's day. Many residents were not aware of the danger of accumulating ash. They lost their roofs. Silvanus has been a very busy worker ever since. Our home is finished now, and we let Silvanus build himself an apartment downstairs. He lives with us now. We share meals, chores, and endless sex in every conceivable combination and position. Longinus and I travel to Rhodes frequently. With a good share of his giant sack of gold, he set up a trade route. In exchange for the now scarce Neapolitan wine (the volcano destroyed many vineyards), he gets Rhodian amphorae, considered the most elegant in the Empire. Many Neapolitan wine sellers want to emphasize the rarity and supremacy of their wine. These amphorae are the finishing touch. I shop for other types of pottery, as well as jewelry. These items, a few denarii for a shipment, are worth dozens of gold coins when we sell them in Naples. We watch our money grow every day. And no longer by magic.

My magic went on hiatus the night of the eruption. At that point, my cock had grown to nearly match

Longinus'; I helped Gastron find a wife, and I needed no magic to do good in the world. My transformation from skinny boy to muscular man continues, but only because, with my newfound strength, it feels good to do heavy physical labors, which naturally causes muscles to grow. With our twin cocks, Silvanus has his pick every night. Greedy as he is, he often picks both.

Several months ago, we found an entrance to an underground crypt on the Decumanus Maiore. We gave the familiar handshake and were welcomed as brothers in the Neapolitan brotherhood. Silvanus joined the cult; he is now a crow. Both Longinus and I ascended from bridegrooms to soldiers. As soldiers, we must always use our magic to bring peace. But our wealth requires very little magic.

Soon after Silvanus's initiation, the magic began. Each time he has an orgasm with one of us inside him, it makes him grow taller and broader, and his muscles become Herculean. He can now drive a peg with a single blow of the hammer. He is building a boat, so the three of us can sail to Rhodes together.

As the three of us sit here on the terrace, looking at the much-diminished mountain and the extraordinary Bay over which it presides, we feel blessed in many ways. Longinus and I found one another; then, we found magic. Silvanus narrowly escaped with his life; now he gets his greedy ass stuffed like forcemeat, then watches his muscles and bones grow like a Titan. He was once shorter than me. Now he is nearly as tall as Longinus and three times as thick with muscle.

We are two escaped slaves and a freedman, living together peaceably, earning money through honest trade. I could not have seen myself in this state two years ago, when I was alone, oppressed, and used by every man and slave in the fullonica and at the piss buckets. If Longinus had not shared that tiny shred of hope and confidence that gave me the courage to introduce myself to Claudius and demand payment, I doubt we would ever have begun our journey to freedom and comfort. We keep no slaves, for, like the Greeks, we find the practice detestable. We pay tradesmen, former slaves, or anyone else with a service we don't know how to do ourselves.

There is something exquisite about the Bay of Neapolis. To see such a vista from our terrace, without fear of a whip or cudgel, is the essence of freedom itself. When I share the panorama with two handsome lovers, I wonder if I might have ascended to the kingdom of heaven that Christ described to his disciples.

The sun is setting over Misenium and the islands of Procida and Ischia. Soon the three of us shall retire to our bed, where we will poke, prod, pound, and pleasure one another until the second watch. And tomorrow, we will take our dirty bedclothes to the fullonica on the Decumanus Superiore, run by a good man with paid laborers and no slaves. That is freedom.

NOTES ABOUT MONEY

At the time Vesuvius erupted, an Aureus constituted a month's pay for a soldier. A denarius was the daily wage for a skilled laborer

Coin — Value
One Aureus – $1,800.00 USD*
Quinarius Aureus – half an Aureus
Denarius — 1/25 an Aureus
Quinarius Argenteus — 1/50 an aureus
Sestertius — 1/100 an aureus
Dupondius — 1/200 an aureus
As — 1/400 an aureus
Semis — 1/800 an aureus
Quadrans — 1/1600 an aureus

*in modern buying power.

NOTES ABOUT
MEASUREMENT

digitus (finger) = 1/16 pes, ¾ of an inch
pollex (thumb) = 1/12 pes, about an inch
palmus (palm width) = 1/4 pes, about 3 inches
palmus major* (palm length) = ¾ pes about 9 inches
pes (foot) = 1 pes about 12 inches
palmipes (foot and a palm) = 1 1/4 pedes about 15 inches
cubitum* (cubit) = 1 1/2 pedes 17-18 inches

*Longinus's astonishing cock was just under one cubitum long and one palmus major in circumference when erect. Even soft, it was over one pes long.

ABOUT PETER SCHUTES

Peter Schutes is a fictional character. He was modeled after the gay pulp fiction authors of the 1970s and 1980s. His creator often wondered who the men were who wrote these books, and so he created Peter to satisfy his curiosity.

Peter was born in 1896 to a wealthy New England family. His whole life, he carried a massive burden: he had a gigantic penis. His sex life was defined by the men who worshipped him.

Peter led a tempestuous life, which is documented in the fictional masterpiece "The Autobiography of Peter Schutes." To learn more about this prolific and prodigious author, we recommend reading his immortal tale of life with too much of a good thing.

OTHER BOOKS FROM PETER SCHUTES PUBLISHING

E-books and Paperbacks (as noted)

The Able Seaman

The Anaconda Copper

The Autobiography of Peter Schutes*

Backwoods Delivery

Big Bodies of All Sizes*

Big Hole River*

Bobbing Buoys and Salty Seamen*

Bunkhouse Buddies*

The Butt Baby*

Cloistered

Confessions of a Rodeo Clown*

Dark as a Dungeon*

Demonic Deception *aka* Deceived, Cursed & Blessed

Desert Island Daddies

The Expectant Member

Firehouse Lovers

The Fish

Five Erotic Tales*

The Gospel of Priapus

Hercules and Lippos

Hobo Honey

Hot Blue Collars*

Hotshot

Logger's Delight

Muscle Bottom*

Panama Heat

Satanic Seductions*

Satan's Sissy Boy

The Thigh Baby

Under the Boardwalk

World's Biggest

Coming Soon

Backwoods Delivery - The Complete Daddy's Boy Series

Like the Greeks Do*

Higher Education*

Hoboes, Hustlers, and Jailbirds*

Small Cockpits and Big Hangars*

Tales of Two Daddies*

*Available as Paperbacks